Riviera Stories
Just Below the Surface

by
Debra Moffitt

Short Stories

Cover and interior design by Damonza

Copyright by Debra Moffitt, 2013

Published by Atma Media, 2013

ISBN-13: 978-0615479132

ISBN-10: 0615479138

Appeasing Kali *was first published by* Cha: Asian Literary Review, *Hong Kong, February, 2008, and* Anthony's Butterfly *was published in the* French Literary Review, *Aude, France, October, 2008.*

Praise for Debra Moffitt's
Books & Writings

"*Like Eat, Pray, Love* without the whine!"

    —Janna McMahan, bestselling author of *Anonymity* and *The Ocean Inside* (About *Garden of Bliss*)

"Debra Moffitt's inspiring book is an oasis in a stressed-out world…I highly recommend it."

    —Mary Alice Monroe, *New York Times* bestselling author of *Beach House Memories* (About *Awake in the World: 108 Ways to Live a Divinely Inspired Life*)

"In traveling the world, we often come home to our most profound truths. In this lushly detailed, luxuriant read of a book, readers are taken on Moffitt's own soul journey: from London to India and beyond, and invited to use dreaming, intuition and synchronicity in their own lives, for extraordinary healing and growth. Highly recommended!"

    —Sara Wiseman, author *Becoming Your Best Self* and *Writing the Divine* (About *Garden of Bliss*)

"Hypnotic and graceful, *Appeasing Kali* explores what it means to pursue spiritual understanding in a land whose countless meanings seem just out of reach."

—Tammy Ho Lai-Ming and Jeff Zroback, Editors, *Cha: An Asian Literary Journal* (on *Appeasing Kali*)

"Debra Moffitt has written a work of pure inspiration. If you want to live a purposeful life, *Garden of Bliss* will show you how to tend your inner garden so that your soul blooms with divine joy."

—Melissa Alvarez, author of *365 Ways to Raise Your Frequency* (About *Garden of Bliss*)

"Through Debra Moffitt's simple stories from her own life, leaping from business executive, to spiritual seeker, to writer, journalist, and now author, she shows us the way to find inner peace in times that appear filled with turmoil....I assure you, you won't be disappointed. It's a gem."

—Sarah Susanka, author of *The Not So Big Life* (About *Awake in the World: 108 Ways to Live a Divinely Inspired Life*)

This is a wonderfully courageous, open, poetic work of soul exploration. Debra guides the reader on the winding pathway of her own soul discovery with vivid, soul-shaping incidents punctuated by equally powerful dreams and inspirations....Love is the watchword; feminine wisdom, the light; and storied narrative, the music. A valuable, intelligent, soulful book."

—Dr. Lee Irwin, Author of *Alchemy of the Soul* and Professor of Religious Studies, College of Charleston (About *Garden of Bliss*)

"Everyone has a secret garden, but few of us are aware of it. That's why it's secret. By inviting you into her garden Debra Moffitt uncovers and unlocks the gate to your own. This is a book for the spiritual gardener eager to till the soil of self and harvest the wisdom of Self."

—Rabbi Rami Shapiro, author of *Writing, The Sacred Art* and columnist for *Spirituality & Health Magazine* (About *Garden of Bliss*)

Other Books by the Author

Awake in the World:
108 Practices to Live a Divinely Inspired Life

Garden of Bliss:
Cultivating the Inner Landscape for Self-Discovery

About the Author

Debra Moffitt is the award-winning author of *Awake in the World* and *Garden of Bliss*. Her writing is deeply influenced by her world travels and living abroad on the French Riviera, and near Lugano, Switzerland. Debra writes in English, French, and Italian, and her articles, essays, and stories appear in publications around the globe. Her fiction was broadcast by BBC World Services Radio and has been published in *Cha: Asian Literary Journal*, and *The French Literary Review*. She leads workshops on writing, creativity, and spirituality in the United States and Europe and is a faculty member of the Esalen Institute and the Sophia Institute. She shares her time between South Carolina and France. Visit her online at www.awakeintheworld.com and www.debramoffitt.com.

"What I wanted to do was to carry my investigations further....we need something more than the satisfaction of vision alone; we need to manifest the world of things unseen."

— Raoul Dufy

Table of Contents

Introduction

When I first moved to Antibes, France I became spellbound by the wealth and glamour. Up and down the French Riviera, Rolls Royces and Ferraris seem commonplace. Van Cleef & Arpels and Cartier display jewels in storefronts worth millions. A yacht in the harbor was rumored to have its name spelled out in giant platinum letters and hung from the ship's deck. Beautiful people stretch out under parasols on private beach mattresses and yearn to meet rock stars and millionaires at exclusive parties. It all looks lovely and happy. But sometimes the cracks in the veneer start to appear and gnawing discontent and disillusionment seep out into the brilliant sunshine.

You begin to see it in the insecure glances that people make as they study their honed appearances in window reflections. It comes across when you see the yacht owner who abandons his exquisite boat to sit in the harbor because he has no time to use it. You see it in the wealthy business owner who collects art but only keeps copies in his home while the originals languish in dark bank vaults. One of the most poignant stories for me was of a man who dreamed of dining at an exclusive five star restaurant where he once worked. He saved up money and got up the courage to go there as a guest. He wanted to be served in the place where he had once served. When he realized his dream, he found that the meal left him hungry, his ex-colleagues snubbed him, and he ultimately felt bitter and broke. The actual experience didn't come anywhere near his dream. It only left him feeling lonely and disgruntled as he dined alone by candlelight under a crystal chandelier in a room full of people he despised. He left scratching his head and wondering if there might be something more enduring and noble in life.

Like this man at the five-star restaurant, other people I met also became disillusioned with the superficial, materialistic craziness. Often when their wild dreams of wealth were fulfilled they felt empty and lonely. Some of them realized there had to be something else. Their dive into material dreams amused and satisfied them for a little while, but in the long term those dreams gave way to feelings of emptiness and a hungering for something more substantial. Many, like me, started to look deeper, and some of us set off on journeys or moved away.

In *Riviera Stories* the surreal and film festival-like atmosphere of the French Riviera reveals a coastline where great wealth and extreme poverty of the spirit walk side by side. In *The Flip Side of Life* this contrast provokes a rock icon, who has lost his motivation to write music to disguise himself under a beard and dirty clothes and go in search of more inspiration anonymously on the street. Observing couples and singles at parties inspired *Secret Garden* where jealousy causes an act of violence. *Unhinged* proves that things are really as crazy as they seem when commuters watch a briefcase-toting businessman lose it along the highway. In *Peaking in Monaco*, a Monaco businessman, who fears falling, meets an attractive rock-climbing amazon and invites her out to dinner where he ends up having to accomplish a death-defying feat to please her. Riviera resident, Caroline, loses herself in men, in *Whispers of the Soul,* and finally begins to find herself and some joy when she travels to India in the closing story, *Appeasing Kali.*

Most of the characters in *Riviera Stories* are at a point of crisis and change. Their desires and relationships have propelled them to explore the material world and experience their desires fully until they reach a place where some of them begin to realize there has to be something more, something beyond all of the beautiful things and appearances. And maybe they choose to begin a search to find out what that might be. This collection of stories set on the *Côte d'Azur* explores the lives of these people as they reach this critical jumping-off point where they're about to begin the journey to discover something more, something maybe even spiritual.

Chapter 1
Secret Garden

"Is it already eight?" Jessica says. She leads Dea up the stone stairway to her kitchen.

Dea hands over a bouquet of white orchids and glances at her watch: 7:45 p.m.

"It's close," she says. Jessica places the flowers in a gold-fleck-ed Murano vase on a side table while Dea stands in the doorway and shifts from foot to foot. The vast rooms with vaulted ceilings and *tommette* floors make Dea feel small.

"You always arrive unfashionably early," Jessica says. She perches on designer high heels and pries open a blue tin can.

"So I can get to bed early, I guess." Dea laughs it off, uncomfortable when anyone asks about deeper motives. While Jessica works with the contents of the can, Dea studies her own reflection in the glass cabinet. Her linen pants and silk knit sweater set contrast with Jessica's mini-skirt and transparent crepe blouse. Dea slides the sweater off and wraps it around her neck leaving her shoulders bare in hopes of being more in tune with Jessica.

"I met someone I like," Jessica says. A sly smile plays on her siliconed, pink lips.

"Will I meet him tonight?"

"He's coming with his wife." Jessica's glossy mouth forms into a grin.

Dea's eyes widen. "You like to live dangerously."

"Do you like caviar?" Jessica scoops the black, shiny eggs into a crystal bowl and licks at the ones that cling to her pearl-nailed fingertip. Her platinum and diamond rings sparkle as she twists her finger from her mouth.

"Well it's...it's okay," Dea says. Scenes of fishermen gutting sturgeons pop into her mind and she feels sorry for the fish. "Can I give a hand?"

"Here. Put these on the ice." Jessica thrusts the bowl at her and points to a long mahogany table in the living room arrayed with linen; champagne in a silver bucket; smoked salmon; fresh vegetables; dips; thin slices of beef *Carpaccio*; and an empty bowl of ice. Dea places the eggs there and slips out to the jasmine-laden terrace behind the sliding glass doors where a fountain gurgles. From behind the glass Dea watches as other guests begin to fill the room. Their mouths form O's like fish in an aquarium as they greet each other and their voices sound distant and muffled as if they speak through water. The scene unfurls in perfect synchronization like a water ballet: the women come together to kiss cheeks then part; the men slap backs or shake hands and pull away. They look as if they are choreographed by some higher force of nature. Dea admires Jessica's ease in the crowd as she flits from guest to guest. After the death of her financier husband six months ago, she moved to Vence to start a new life. Jessica embraced the Riviera like a willing bride embraces her new husband. She invited it in by throwing frequent cocktail parties, holding exclusive luncheons, and doing charity work. She hoped desperately to meet another man. Her wealth and natural warmth provide oil to stoke the social fires.

Dea slips quietly inside the room, but stays near the wall with her arms crossed over her chest. She feels like a foreign body, a meteor or a shooting star, drifting through the space between them with no one strong enough to capture her in their orbit. A champagne glass on the buffet attracts her attention, and she picks it up and clings to it like an amulet that she hopes will admit her into their club and give her a sense of belonging. One man wears a plaid sports jacket and boasts of his stock market trades to Jessica. But she excuses herself and coaxes Dea to the center of the room.

"This is Dea. She's a writer," Jessica says to the group. The people are mostly Americans, but some French neighbors and a few Brits make up the crowd too. A suave, olive-skinned man with almond shaped eyes and broad shoulders moves closer to Dea. "She took me to meet a Nobel Prize winning poet in Monaco last weekend." Dea's cheeks flush and she tries to slip away. She hates being the center of attention, but Jessica holds her elbow in a firm grasp. "He read some poems about Americans to us. What was that one called, Dea?" Dea peers wide-eyed into the crowd of thirty or so people. She feels like a deer standing in a car's headlights; she's unable to speak, but she doesn't want to disappoint her friend. "You recited it earlier. Remember?" The crowd remains silent, expectant. *The Continental Divide – an abyss in the midst of the American's heart...,* Dea thinks and swallows. The words remain blocked inside. She clears her throat, takes a deep breath, and faces the crowd.

"Uh, no," she says her voice barely audible.

"Well, Dea's a little otherworldly. She spends a lot of time in her inner world. I guess that's what makes her a good writer," Jessica announces. She seems perplexed at Dea's social unease. Without missing a beat Jessica glides smoothly away to open another bottle of champagne. Dea curls her shoulders forward and backs away from the center of the room. 'Otherworldly'? she thinks. Her brows knit together. The conversations around her return to stock markets, fashion, and sports. Jessica refills the champagne glass of the olive-skinned man and looks longingly into his eyes. The woman beside him crosses her arms and cocks her head to one side, jealously taking in every gesture and glance between them. Her eyes cut into them like lasers. Jessica leads the man toward Dea.

"I'd like you to meet Amar," Jessica says.

"Oh, yes. I've already heard about you," Dea says enthusiastically. She reaches out to shake his hand. Jessica shoots a warning look, and Dea's natural enthusiasm fades. The woman at Amar's side seems like a weight bound to him by a thick invisible cord.

"Dea, you may be the youngest woman here," he says. She scans the room and shrugs her shoulders.

"Could be." She is at least ten years younger than the others.

"How lucky you are. So young and beautiful." He pauses and turns slightly to the woman at his side. "This is Laurence…" He hesitates, clears his throat. "…my wife." Laurence glares hatefully.

"*Bonsoir*," she hisses. Her mouth puckers into a tight, angry O when she says the word.

"*Enchantée*," Dea says politely, ignoring the darkness in Laurence's voice.

"Laurence was a diplomat, but they made her redundant, as the Brits say." Amar seems to relish the words. Laurence scowls and slinks away to a couch next to an elderly couple. "She's from an aristocratic family and needs to be put in her place sometimes," he confesses. Amar steps close enough to Dea that she can feel his hot breath. He stares intently at her bare shoulder, and she puts on her sweater to cover her skin. But his warm dark eyes continue to explore every inch and curve of her without apologies or embarrassment. She wants to disappear, but Jessica stands near the door making it difficult to slip away without appearing rude.

"Oh," Dea says not knowing how to respond to such a blunt description of his wife's failure.

"I want to write too," Amar says. "Fiction, I mean."

"What?" she says distracted. Dea focuses intently on the door waiting for Jessica to leave the exit clear for her to escape.

"I wrote a book too." He reaches out with his finger and casually touches the curl of long hair that lies on her arm. She steps away and out of his reach. "But I want to write stories about people now."

"Oh, that's nice. What are you writing?"

"My first book was on men who are abused by women, by their wives." She realizes he is serious and turns her focus from the door to his face. "I've done a study on this." Dea studies his wife who stands a few feet in front of them with a small group of women. Laurence maneuvers uncomfortably around the women, as if she's trying to find her place among the socialites and wealthy Americans. Her face is narrow and sharp. Her eyes are hard and sharp, and her body appears thin and sharp. They are accented by pointy-toed shoes and narrow black pants. A crisp Hermès scarf hangs around her neck. She looks like someone who could inflict some real damage on a man's ego.

"Okay," Dea finally yields. "Tell me about it." He seems happy that he finally has her full attention.

"Not here," he says. "Let's get together later on." She looks at his wife, then back at him. "Don't worry about my wife. We have an arrangement."

"Oh, you're making her redundant too?" she says. He laughs.

"Life is complicated," he sighs. "See, I love my house here in Vence, but if we divorce she wants to take it from me out of spite." Dea sips from her glass and waits for more. "I don't know why she can't be satisfied with the house in the country."

"Mmm," she muses.

"And so I'm free, more or less," he says apologetically, as if she should understand.

"It sounds like less rather than more," Dea says.

"Why's it so complicated?"

"My life's pretty simple," she says.

"Single?"

"Absolutely." She has no intention of changing this vital statistic anytime soon, especially with a married man.

"That makes it easier," he says. "You know, writer to writer, maybe I could learn some things from you. Why don't we get together again soon?"

"We'll see."

"Check me out with Jessica," he says. "She'll give me a good reference." Dea scans the room and catches Jessica looking at them.

"Hmmm, think so?" Dea says. Laurence steps up to the table behind Amar and stabs at some olives. When she turns, her eyes connect with Dea's. Laurence bumps Amar's right elbow, splashing his champagne down the front of Dea's white silk sweater.

"Oh forgive me," Amar says as he dabs at the drops around the V of her neck. She takes the napkin from him to wipe away the rest. Laurence looks sideways at her, apparently satisfied with her aim, but irritated by his attention. He turns around. "Oh, you again," he mutters. Laurence's dark eyes harden into a squint. But Amar picks up another napkin and he continues to make a fuss. "Here, let me help." He touches the napkin to her heart where the sweater clings to her curves.

"The French say it's good luck to be baptized in champagne," she says lightly.

"Yes, you should put a touch behind your ears too," Amar adds. He reaches out to put a damp finger there under Dea's dark hair, but she casually dodges his attempt by reaching for more napkins.

"Thanks to Laurence, I'm now wearing eau de champagne," she says. Laurence scowls again and walks away.

"Dear Dea," Amar says. "You must forgive us." He looks at her breasts. Jessica stands at Amar's elbow now surveying the scene.

"Would you like to change into one of my blouses?" she offers.

"That's kind. But no. Really, it'll be fine. Excuse me. I'd like to find the ladies room."

"You know where it is," Jessica motions toward the door. When Dea reaches the hallway, the fresh air fills her with an urge for freedom and she slips out leaving the hum of the party behind.

***

Dea calls Jessica the next day to say thanks for her gracious hospitality. Jessica is her usual warm and bubbly self and doesn't seem to mind that Dea left early.

"Amar seems like an intriguing man," Dea says. Jessica clears her throat.

"You met his wife too?"

"Laurence? Yes."

"He says he can't afford a divorce since he left the World Bank."

"Oh, that's unfortunate."

"We've talked about it. I told him that money is not an issue," Jessica says. "But, of course that would mean we'd live at least part of the year in the U.S." Jessica is a fortunate widow who inherited millions, and freeing Amar of his disagreeable burden would be as easy for her as it would be for most people to give a few pennies to a beggar.

"He's very charming. You would make a good couple. He'd fit in well with your cosmopolitan New York crowd." Dea reassures

Jessica.

"I think so too," she says. "Are you free for lunch on Thursday?"

Dea scans the agenda by the phone. "Yes."

"Oh, good. Amar's very interested in writing now and he'd like to talk with you. It'll just be the three of us."

"That sounds nice."

"Come at twelve-thirty. I'm looking forward to it."

"Me too," Dea says and hangs up.

***

Dea arrives five minutes late this time to make up for her inadvertent social error of usually arriving too early. Amar answers the doorbell, kisses her once on each cheek in the local French fashion, a little too close to her mouth, and escorts her to the dining room where Jessica puts salad plates on the table. A shoulder-high vanilla scented candle flickers in the center of the room, even though the Riviera sunlight floods in through the sliding glass doors. The scent of jasmine wafts in from the flowers hanging over the trellises on the terrace. Some lotus grow in a small pool filled with papyrus. The fountain gurgles peacefully. Jessica bends down to kiss Dea's cheeks and smiles. "You're making progress. You arrived five minutes late," she says.

"I'm glad you recognize my efforts to be more socially accept-able," Dea says.

Jessica wears a blue-jean mini-skirt that reveals her long, tan legs, and Dea wonders if she was ever a fashion model. Jessica once confessed that as a good Catholic girl, she waited to marry before losing her virginity at the age of 24. But now, driven by lone-liness and desire, she is ready to break the rules. Most men would jump at the chance. She's charming and shapely. Back home she moves among financiers, movie directors, and film stars. But Amar seems indifferent, at least around Dea. Jessica asks her to sit at one end of the oval table and seats Amar at the opposite end.

"I'd rather sit between you two," he says, protesting. Jessica hesitates.

"Okay." She tries to keep her tone neutral, but a bit of irritation seeps through. She sits down opposite Dea and touches Amar's hand as a sign of affection and ownership. But he pulls away and proposes a toast.

"To love and writing," he says. His eyes glitter with desire and longing. His head turns toward Dea. Jessica touches his elbow as a reminder of her presence.

"How about to love of writing," Dea corrects him.

"I'd be happy just to toast to love," Jessica says. "Does anything else matter?" A hint of loneliness sneaks out from behind her well-crafted social mask, but she quickly repairs the cracks and appears happy, light, and self-sufficient again. They chat about literature, but avoid the really interesting things that linger in the air. Things like whether Amar will accept Jessica's offer and divorce; whether Jessica will get what she wants out of it; and whether they will live happily ever after. Dea talks about her work in film and then Amar takes over.

"I have an idea about a woman who falls in love with the wrong man. Everyone and everything in her house, the hairdryer, the washer, the coffeemaker, and even her car, conspire to get rid of him."

"Sounds original," Dea says. "I like it."

"I have an idea too," Jessica adds. "Everything looks so pretty and perfect where I lived, but underneath…" Her voice trails off. Dea recalls Jessica's descriptions of the upper class milieu with mansions full of money and misery. "I saw another side of it when my husband died. Back-stabbing business partners. Greedy children." She shakes her head.

"It could be interesting," Dea says and thinks of a soap opera. Amar sighs and seems bored.

"For dessert, we're having pear sorbet with Poire William liqueur," Jessica says and steps out to the kitchen. Amar perks up, slips his hand under the table and squeezes Dea's knee. She flinches.

"I thought you were dessert," he whispers, then raises his voice as if in response to Jessica. "What a delicious proposition." He smiles at Dea with a look of lust in his eye. "I can't wait."

"I'm not on the menu," Dea whispers back and flicks his hand away.

"With a little warmth you'll soften up just like the sorbet. I bet you'd melt...," he whispers again. His eyes penetrate hers and he leans back.

"Sounds messy," she says, and frowns. Jessica returns beaming, with a tray in her hands.

"Oh, so you're finally going to accept one of my propositions," Jessica says to Amar, bending over him to set a bowl on the table so that her breasts are visible under her low-cut blouse. He chuckles. Dea looks at him perplexed and wants to know more, not because he is handsome (which he is and knows it), but simply out of curiosity. Human nature fascinates her, and she wants to understand what makes him tick. But Jessica has that look of love in her eyes, and Dea knows it's time to go. She excuses herself and leaves the two of them alone.

***

Amar calls Dea several times before she finally accepts his lunch invitation. He says he found her number at Jessica's and wants to cook for her at his beloved home. So when she arrives, he prepares sole fillets in butter, Provençale style tomatoes, and *crème brulée* with sprigs of lavender on top. It is exquisite, a delight for the senses. When only a centimeter of Ott rosé remains in the bottle, she asks him about the sensitive subject of his career. He is only 50, an early age to retire.

"Why did you leave the World Bank?" she says. He sips some wine and clears his throat. A bitter look crosses his face.

"It was politics, you know." She listens intently and concentrates on his face and eyes. He crosses his fingers together and leans back. "I was at the peak of my career, but others were jealous. They forced me out."

"Sounds like they made you redundant too," she says. He frowns.

"I hadn't anticipated it would turn out like this."

"Nothing ever does," she says in a gentler tone. "Nothing ever turns out like we imagine."

"No I guess not," he says. "Now, I'm stuck without much money. Laurence wants the house and just about everything else. But this house is mine. It's like part of my soul. Let me give you a tour." He shows her each room of the house: the blue ceramic tiled kitchen that looks like the walls of a Babylonian temple, the white marble bath with ornate gold-plated faucets, the sitting room with Kilim carpets and silk pillows. Amar lives in luxury surrounded by antique objects from his Persian past, and his place has a slow, lazy Middle-Eastern feel about it. A ceiling fan stirs the air and beats out a steady, constant rhythm that joins with their footsteps to fill the hall as they walk over the bare stone floors. He loves and cares for the place as if it is an extension of himself. His father's drawings of Persia hang on the walls; his mother's hand-woven fabrics cover the sitting room couch, and his uncle's gold tipped cane leans in one corner. A sword hangs in the stairwell. It belonged to a great uncle who fought in a war. Amar presents every room, until they reach his painting room where boxes of well used pastels and charcoals sit open on a table. A charcoal and pastel drawing of a lovely, naked woman with long, dark hair and red lips also sits on the table. Dea picks it up. A man sits at the woman's feet.

"This one is recent," he says.

"Beautifully done."

"Yes, it's one of my best. I think it's some kind of domination fantasy, a desire for a woman I can surrender to totally."

"It sounds dangerous. You're looking for a goddess or something?"

"She's no fantasy. Don't you see?"

The woman looks uncannily like herself. "Oh," she says. Her cheeks flush. Amar looks down, his eyes glistening. She is suddenly, acutely aware of the heat from his body and that he is standing too close. He takes the drawing from her hand and puts it on the table. She steps back and hopes to disappear. But he moves closer. She backs up again until her heels touch the wall. His breathing changes. It's faster and more shallow. A shiver runs down Dea's spine. The air feels heavy and hot, charged with electricity, and she holds her breath. Her heart pounds hard, and she feels like a hunted animal looking down the barrel of a loaded gun.

"Where's your wife?" she says.

He laughs. "She's no threat. She's out at the beach."

"Hmm, I see," Dea says, like a psychoanalyst. If she manages to escape from Amar's charm, then she imagines she will probably not get away from Laurence's ire. "I've got to go."

"You don't know what you're missing."

"Laurence can fill me in on the details next time we meet," she says. He lights a Player's cigarette and leans against the wall with the tip smoldering. Thick, heavy smoke fills the air. "But I told you we have an agreement." She crosses her arms over her chest.

"You might have an agreement. I'm not so sure she does," Dea says. He snorts and looks out the window.

"Well, let me know if you change your mind. But don't wait too long. Otherwise, the window of opportunity may close." He smiles and his white teeth contrast with his dark skin. Dea walks to the front door and he follows. The moment she stands on the doorstep outside she starts to breathe freely again.

"What about Jessica?" she says.

"Oh that," he says looking down toward her house. "I'm not for sale."

"But she's attractive. She maybe even loves you." He doesn't respond. "You're an interesting case, Amar. I hope you'll share your writing with me anyway." It is a consolation prize, an offer of friendship and camaraderie rather than the more ephemeral status of lover. He agrees he will and leans down to kiss her cheeks. "For the rest, get divorced first, and then we'll see."

"I know," he says, playfully clasping her elbow. "I'll divorce Laurence, marry Jessica, and take you as my lover." She rolls her eyes.

"You may be handsome Amar, but you're not worth the misery." He stands there smiling seductively and seems flattered that she called him handsome. She waves goodbye, takes off her sandals, and nearly runs down the stone steps to flee the tension. The smooth warm granite caresses the bottoms of her feet, and she exits Amar's garden gate onto the cobblestone street. At an angle, she sees Jessica unlocking her front door. She puts her head down and scurries away through a side street. When Dea's out in the sun on the main street again, she takes a few steps then stops short. A dark-haired woman who resembles Laurence appears at the street corner. Dea turns around and heads down the opposite street, past the ancient church by the gurgling fountain, past the Gault & Millau acclaimed restaurant, and down the cobblestone street to a parking lot loaded with tourists. She drives home through the summer traffic and down to the sea where she dives off of the white cliffs on the Cap d'Antibes. The warm, salty seawater washes away the tension and calms her nerves. She stretches out on the rocks awhile and seeks to understand human nature. When no answers come she heads home to sleep a deep, peaceful sleep far from the madness of people.

***

A couple of weeks later, Jessica calls Dea about another party. Recently back from the Seychelles and St. Tropez, she wants to celebrate her birthday with a crowd of friends. Amar and Laurence come together as a package this time. Amar complains of a headache and announces he will leave. He kisses Laurence, his wife, dutifully on the cheek, followed by Jessica who turns her head just in time for his kiss to land on her lips. She smiles slyly, then apologizes but doesn't mean it. When he comes around to Dea who stands next to them, he grasps her head and kisses her passionately. Dea pushes him away and gasps. He smiles, content with himself. Laurence and Jessica stare wild-eyed at her.

"Uh," Dea says pushing him away and wiping her mouth with disgust. Amar sounds cool and remote. "I love you," he says loud enough for the others to hear, and walks out the door. She pauses an instant, confused. Laurence and Jessica glare at her. Their eyes blame her and make her feel guilty, but for what? How can she explain Amar's strange behavior to them she wonders, but her mind goes blank. She walks to the buffet and hopes the two women will shift their attention someplace else. Dea fills a plate with scallops and fresh vegetables, and sits down alone at a table. Laurence sits down casually beside her as if nothing has happened, but darkness fills her face. Dea slides her chair a few inches away. A group of strangers join them and introduce themselves. Laurence remains ominously silent and threatening. A kind man asks Dea what she writes. In a few minutes, the whole group at the table turns to listen to her talk about a film project she's working on for Disney. This adds to Laurence's heavy brooding, and when the conversation shifts to someone else, Laurence speaks in French, a language that the others will not understand.

"You're nothing but a phantom, a ghost," she hisses. "Why does Jessica invite you to her parties? You don't belong here." Her eyes turn hard and her face puckers as if she has just bitten into a sour green plum. From the wrinkles around her lips, it is clear that this is a favorite expression that she often wears. Dea looks stunned, speechless.

"Pardon me?"

"*Tu n'es rien.* You're nothing. No one," she hisses. Shock ripples through Dea. She begins to sympathize with Amar and understand the kind of violence he wrote about. "Among all of these wealthy people, you're like dust. You're invisible. You have no money, no status." Dea's face flushes with embarrassment, and she looks away trying to find the right word to make light of the accusations. "*I* am a diplomat," Laurence says.

"Were," Dea mutters. She looks at the door to plan a safe escape.

"*I* am somebody. *You* are not." Laurence hisses.

Dea does not know how to disarm the hostile human being, which has been set in motion before her eyes like a bomb about to explode. Dea turns to the couple beside her and smiles, hoping they will offer a way out. But Laurence continues to attack in hostile French.

"Listen," Dea says finally. "I'm not having an affair with your husband, if that's what you think. I don't know why Amar kissed me. Maybe you're not giving him enough."

"It's nothing to do with that." Laurence trembles, and rage fills her eyes. "You should know your place in society and keep it."

Dea takes a deep breath and focuses on dipping a fresh carrot into an herb sauce on her plate. "Hate isn't diplomatic and it's certainly not very attractive, especially for a woman. It'll give you more wrinkles." She connects with Laurence's eyes and lets the words sink in. "It might help you calm down if you drink a glass of cold water. Or perhaps you should leave. Go lie down and you'll feel better," Dea says. She speaks calmly, evenly with tight self-control.

Laurence's face turns red and her eyes bulge like a mad woman's. "How dare you suggest that I be the one to go. I'm no ghost. Are you implying I'm a ghost?" She takes her knife and fork and jabs at the raw beef *Carpaccio* on her plate. A drop of blood drips from it as she lifts a piece to her lips. But her hunger seems to remain unsatisfied. When her fork is empty she glares at Dea. With deliberate aim, she rams the fork down on the back of Dea's right hand and cuts across it with her knife. She slices the soft flesh between Dea's thumb and index finger as if she plans to consume it.

A woman screeches. Dea's blood oozes onto the white linen tablecloth. Her mouth falls open. But no sound emerges. Like an injured animal, Dea looks for a way to escape, but a crowd gathers around her. Dea feels a moment of shock and panic. Fear, anxiety, and hurt rise in waves and threaten to engulf her if she does not get out of here fast and find a refuge. But she sees no exit and the circle of people encroach more tightly to stare. So she escapes inward, back inside, into herself. She becomes aware of standing at the threshold of a deep inner sanctuary. It looks inviting like a tranquil garden. In her imagination, she crosses into this safe haven and a wave of peace sweeps through her. From that quiet, inner place, she watches the blood flow out of her hand; a woman's face turns pale; people's mouths move as they speak, but their words do not reach her. She stays deep inside away from the pain, conscious of something that is solid and eternal, something that transcends the madness of the outer world. She lingers there for a while, an eternity it seems. A placid, Buddha-like trance crosses her face until she finally steps out of the serene elegance and back into the whirring, buzzing cocktail party again.

"Oh my god," she gasps. She automatically stands, wraps a napkin around her hand and cups it to her heart, then opens the napkin a little to peer at the damage. It looks as if a wildcat ripped at her flesh with its claws. One of the guests at the table clutches a hand over her mouth and looks faint. Dea cradles her injured hand like a baby next to her chest and turns to Laurence. Her remorseless eyes stare up at Dea and then dart away. "I've got to go," Dea says.

"Don't let her get away with that," a man at the table says. "I mean swear at her or something." Someone alerts Jessica and she brings bandages and disinfectant. Laurence continues to eat her beef undisturbed. No apologies. No reaction. Nothing.

"I'd press charges," another man yells with an intoxicated slur. "I'd have my lawyer sue her for every penny. She's inhuman."

Dea glances at her hand and then back at Laurence again, wondering how anyone could inflict such harm. It looks as if no soul is at home behind the window of Laurence's eyes. The empty look sends a chill through Dea. Laurence tidily folds and places her linen napkin on the table and struts out the door.

"Call an ambulance!" a woman in a chiffon dress croaks.

"I'll take care of this," Jessica says. She towers over Dea and pushes her back down into her seat. Jessica mechanically opens the first aid box, pulls on surgical gloves to avoid contact with the blood, and douses a strip of cotton with rubbing alcohol. Then she attacks the bloody cut, rubbing fiercely. Dea winces, but Jessica focuses intently on the wounds and avoids eye contact.

"Laurence is mad," Dea says.

"You kissed her husband," Jessica reminds her.

The pain in her hand throbs brutally, and Jessica rubs away each new spurt of blood until the flesh feels sensitive and raw. "Go gentle on me." She breathes in a sharp breath. "He kissed *me*, Jessica."

"Looked like you kissed him," Jessica says. Her breath is tight and jerky as if she is working hard to stay in control and maybe not cry. She roughly scrubs the wounds with the burning disinfectant. Dea feels numb. "How could you?" she accuses.

"But I didn't," Dea protests. A tear wells up in the corner of Jessica's eye.

"Doesn't it hurt?" she says finally as she wraps a bandage tightly around Dea's hand.

"Not as much as you do. Are you sleeping with him?"

"We'd finally worked it out." She digs a clasp into the gauze to close it. "He'd agreed to divorce and stayed over." She chokes back tears.

"Did Laurence know?"

"I think so. Yes."

"He's playing games with you," Dea says, and I'm the scapegoat she thinks.

Jessica releases her hand and steps back. She stares so coldly that her eyes could turn Dea to dry ice. "I am so sorry," she says. Hints of anger steeped with sadness leak into Jessica's voice. Then she stiffens, regains control and puts on the cool, distant smile of a hostess with everything under control and clears her throat. "Another glass of champagne?"

"No thanks." Dea just wants to escape the madness. She knows now why she keeps mostly to herself. People are too unpredictable and painful. She walks out and drives home to nurse her wounds in the safety of solitude.

At home, Dea turns out the lights in her bedroom and opens

the glass doors to feel the sea breeze. A scotch filled with crushed ice sits on the night table, and she sips it to drive away the throbbing hurt and numb the ache in her heart. It only makes it worse, and her tears flow. In the darkness, wracked with pain, she turns inside for refuge and becomes aware of that inner sanctuary again, the garden of peace. She crosses the threshold and lingers in the stillness, grateful to the pain for having driven her into this new discovery. A feeling of contentment fills her, and in an instant she falls asleep.

***

Amar comes by the next day despite Dea's protests. She keeps him outside on her little terrace. For a moment they stand in silence and stare out at the sea and the boats bobbing in Antibes' big harbor. She finishes a cup of thick, black espresso, and refuses to speak to him.

"Laurence said you didn't even react. No anger. No tears. It was like you just sat back and observed the whole scene totally unaffected by it," he muses. "That really made her angry. Maybe I'll try it next time."

"It's your fault," she says finally.

"It was just a little joke. I thought it was funny," he says chuckling to himself.

"It doesn't feel funny." She grimaces. "You wanted them to think we were having an affair. And I paid the price."

"Can I see it?" He points to her hand. She shrugs and lets him unwind the gauze. The air touches the fresh wound and her hand throbs. He winces.

"That's what happens when you play with people's feelings," Dea says.

"This is a first. Laurence usually limits herself to breaking glass." Amar re-wraps her wound and replaces her hand on her lap. "When Laurence hurts me sometimes I'd like to kill her. Don't you want to get even?" She shakes her head no.

"Seems like there's been enough hurt already."

"You're different than most of us," he says. "You just go inside, into your *jardin secret*."

"My *jardin secret?*"

She immediately knows what he means. "My secret garden," she repeats to herself and realizes that this is the place where the pain drove her to, the place where everything remained peaceful, pristine, and pure while the whole world around her was nothing but pain. She only just discovered it, but he named it so casually, so easily, as if anyone might stumble upon it or find it there on a whim.

"The kiss wasn't bad, huh?" he says like a school boy fishing for compliments. She doesn't respond. "Maybe you changed your mind about me?" She shakes her head in disbelief.

"Do you know how much pain you caused?"

"I thought that kiss might inspire you," his voice fades out as he loses confidence.

"It didn't."

She knows Amar will never offer her any sanctuary, or joy, or friendship. No one can, not permanently. But the memories of her secret garden linger on. She wants to return to it, wants to know more. It feels like the place where her heart's desires will find real fulfillment and joy. He turns to go, but she stops him.

"Does everyone have a secret garden?"

"Most people do, but they don't know it," he says. "You must be one of the lucky few." Funny, she thinks as he walks away. Sometimes it's pain that drives the big discoveries. For a moment she feels grateful to Amar, Jessica, and Laurence. Without their madness she might not have been pushed inward to cross into this new frontier of herself. She takes a deep breath and smiles a little. Soon she will return inside again to explore the mystical, secret garden of her soul.

Chapter 2
Unhinged

"You know, I thought I heard camels this morning," Fred says, holding lightly to the steering wheel of his old Volvo. Abdul squints at him and a concerned look comes down over his face like a metal grate. This is the French Riviera, not a circus. He glances at Maya over the seat. She shrugs, half asleep. The traffic slows to a crawl.

"Not again," Abdul complains. "If we leave at 7:45 we avoid this mess." The three commuters sit inside the square box of a car while Fred drives slowly, deliberately toward Sophia Antipolis Hi-Tech Park, the French Silicon Valley.

"It's her fault," Fred says jabbing his thumb over the seat at Maya who sits straddled over the hump in the backseat. Their eyes meet in the rearview mirror and a pout curls out on her lips.

"*Mais non,*" she says. "The curling iron overheated and blew a fuse in the house. Nothing worked. Not even the espresso machine. I couldn't leave without coffee."

"So she made me stop at McDonalds before picking you up." Fred speaks with a British accent, and fingers his counterfeit Omega watch that he picked up in San Remo.

"Ehh. McDonalds serves juice from dirty socks, not coffee," Abdul spouts.

Maya holds both of her hands wrapped around the paper cup and peers out the window. "Oh *mon dieu*! My God," she says with a heavy French accent so that the words sound like *my got*. "Look at that."

Fred downshifts and his eyes dart over to a man walking along the roadside. The man wears a crisp, dry-cleaned suit and silk tie. He grips a brown leather briefcase in his right hand. His eyes stare straight ahead and he moves forward with determined strides.

"He only has on one shoe," Fred says and stiffens.

"It makes him limp," Abdul says.

"Watch!" Maya yelps with excitement. The suited and tied man yanks at a shoe lace, jerks at his remaining shoe, and tosses it aside. "Liberated!" Maya squeals with delight and laughs. "I've always wanted to do that."

"You're an exhibitionist." Fred says then his eyes squint together as he focuses on the man. His black, polished shoe lands in a clump of weeds.

"It looked brand new. I hate to see a man throw away a perfectly good sole," Abdul says.

"I think I know him," Fred gasps. "He looks like someone I used to work with."

"Do you think he's going postal? I hope he doesn't have a gun," Abdul adds.

Fred slows the car to the pace of the walking man who jerks angrily at his tie. The cars behind honk. One man passes and leans on his horn jerking his angry fist in the air at Fred. But other cars gather and brake and slow to a crawl too. The man on foot ignores them all. He reaches up, loosens the tie in a back and forth motion and holds it up to let the wind carry it away. The tie's long silky tail trails in the sea breeze like the tail of a happy kite flashing yellow, red, green, and blue.

"That looked like a Versace tie to me," Fred says.

"Want to go after it?" Abdul says. Fred watches the tie float away in the rearview mirror. "I've always wanted one," he moans with regret. Maya begins to hum the strippers' song.

"Dah da da, dah da da dah...He's not bad." Curlicue hair frames the man's determined face.

"Wah," Abdul says. "His doors have come unhinged." He places his hands together. "Oh Allah. The Imam says it's the comet. It will make some go mad with its serpentine tail. It makes humans feel small and finite and insignificant in the order of things. Then they come unhinged."

"A nice theory," Fred says. "I saw that comet for the first time this morning." He points into the sky toward the East where its faint trace still remains visible. "Isn't it supposed to spray some sort of gaseous matter and debris into our atmosphere that will affect crops and change our weather patterns?"

"My tarot card reader said it's a good omen. Now people who were last will be first and people who were first will be last," Maya says. "With a name like Zamini, I've always been last, so I'm looking forward to it. Maybe I'll even get to sit in the front seat now."

"I get carsick if I sit in back," Abdul says.

"I told Jacqueline about the camels," Fred says. "She said, 'no, you're crazy, can't be camels and pulled the sheet over her head. But you know she was right. When I went to the window I saw they were dromedaries instead."

Abdul looks preoccupied as he studies Fred's drawn face. His eyes meet Maya's again and she raises her eyebrows. Then he turns to see the walking man who holds his grey pin-striped jacket above his head on his index finger until the stiff wind lifts it and carries it off behind him. The jacket puffs up, as if an invisible man inhabits it, and then it hurls its arms around the trunk of a palm tree and seems to hold on tight.

"Dromedaries, huh?" Abdul says.

"One hump, not two, you know," Fred says.

Maya takes out her pack of cigarettes. "Camels have one hump," she insists and holds up the pack to prove it.

"No," Fred says turning to her with a serious face. "They got it wrong."

"Yeah, but think of it," Abdul says. "Who would smoke a pack of Dromedaries? It wouldn't be cool." The traffic picks up again and Fred accelerates.

Maya rolls her eyes. "I am going to check."

"Look at that guy." Fred points now. "He's not going to stop."

"No, but you'd better," Abdul warns nervously.

Fred turns and hits the brake just in time, jerking all of them forward. "Sorry, guys." The line of cars screeches to a halt one by one. The walking man yanks off a sock and sends it flying. "Looks like a crash up front. Now we're stuck. Why's it always like this when you're in a hurry?" Fred laments. "I guess it used to be worse on the M1 outside of London, so I can't complain."

"It's our fate. The Imam says we get what we deserve. No way out."

"*Mais non*," Maya whines. "That's not right. It's karma. What you do comes back to you and hits you in the face. If you do bad, you get a wave of bad. If you do good it comes back around to you too. So you have to do good things."

"Same thing," Fred says. "Different words. When I stepped out of the apartment this morning I saw elephants too."

Abdul's brows crinkle up in worry lines as he eyes Fred. "Man, are you alright?"

"Sure, why?"

"Camels and elephants. I mean this is the French Riviera, not Outer Mongolia," Abdul says.

"I think he drank too much. Isn't that when people see pink camels and elephants?" Maya says, pasting silvery-pink gloss on her mouth and smacking her lips together.

"They weren't pink," Fred says.

Abdul frowns, worried about Fred. Maybe he's coming unhinged too. He lifts his wrist to check the time. "We're going to be late, man. I'm going to get out and start walking too. Just like him," Abdul says. He points to the walking man passing them all. The man pulls his shirt out of his pants and unbuttons it with a look of intense determination.

"If you decide to walk to work at least keep your clothes on," Fred says to the walking man. He cranes his neck to see ahead. "Whoa, looks like we're going to be stuck here awhile." The cars in both lanes stop dead. But the walking man keeps going full steam ahead. He doesn't veer left or right. He walks as if he's the only one in the world. The walking man raises his arm and his unbuttoned shirt flies out like a flag. He shifts the briefcase to the other arm and lets the Mistral wind whip off his shirt and carry it up into the sky. Then suddenly – CRASH – from behind.

"Ha, ha," Fred chuckles. "Look at that." A huge white delivery truck with block letters "COSMOS – *Poisson Frais et Congelé*, Fresh and Frozen Fish," lurches up in the mirror, maybe ten cars back. It smashes the bumper of the last motionless car in the line of traffic and pushes it head on into the car in front. But it doesn't stop there. The force creates a chain reaction pushing car bumper into fender – *Wham, Crunch, Bham* – all the way down the line of blocked vehicles. Fred stops laughing and tries frantically to pull out of the line to the side as he watches the cars lurch toward them in his rearview mirror.

"Oh no. It's coming at us," he panics and locks his foot on the brake.

Abdul twists his head around, then prays *"En ch'Allaah."* Metal crunches, and Maya cries and trembles.

"Let me out," she screams and reaches for the door handle. The sound travels toward them diminishing in power as it approaches. But before she can leap out, the impact reaches the Volvo ramming it from behind and into the car in front. Their heads jerk forward and whip back. Then everything falls silent and motion stops.

Fred rubs his neck. "You guys okay?"

"Yeah," they mumble in unison.

He steps out of the car to examine the damage. The fronts of the cars behind him look like Pekinese dog snouts and their trunks resemble accordions. But his big boxy car shows no trace of any damage. He secretly rejoices at his good fortune. He glances at the irate drivers emerging from their cocoons of cars and cursing the COSMOS truck driver.

"Didn't you see us?" the woman closest to the COSMOS driver screams, a trickle of blood at the corner of her head. "You could have killed us." The truck driver shrugs and points at the walking man who walks ahead bare-chested with his arms outstretched to the wind.

"It's his fault."

"How can it be his fault? He wasn't even driving," a man with a head as smooth as a bowling ball yells. He bounds toward the truck driver with his fist on a taut spring ready to explode into action. The COSMOS man takes refuge in the cab of his truck and locks the door. A cop siren screeches up from behind them, and two guys on police motor bikes pull off their helmets and begin to organize the scene. The truck driver rolls down his window.

"Go arrest that man," he says, pointing at the walking man who unleashes his belt and unzips his pants. The walking man's other hand still clings tightly to the brown brief case. His pinstriped suit pants fall to the ground and he steps out of them.

"It's his fault."

"What do you think he has in his briefcase?" Fred says stepping back in the car and looking at the walking man.

"How's the car?" Abdul worries that he may have to find another ride to work tomorrow.

"It's a Volvo," Fred says. "Not even a scratch."

"A boring car," Maya says.

"But sturdy and safe," Abdul adds. Fred smiles, satisfied.

"Hey!" one cop yells at the walking man. But the walking man steams ahead wearing only his underwear. "Hey wait! Stop!"

"Oh man, he's gonna go all the way," Maya says with excitement. The walking man hooks his thumb into the elastic of his baby-blue Calvin Klein style underwear and they drop to his knees. Then with a flick of his ankle the underwear flies onto the top of a bush and hangs there forlorn. Maya begins to applaud and yip. "Woo, woo," she yells at him. *Encore, encore.* But he is in his own world and seems to hear no one, not the pretty pink-lipped French girl, nor the stern cop. They watch through the windshield as a crowd of people involved in the pileup gather around the policemen. Some point at the naked man, others look tense and worried. One woman bites a fingernail. A few begin to applaud.

"I will tell the Imam," Abdul insists. "It's the unhinging of the whole Western world. No devotion. No love for God. Man's heart is empty like a black hole, as wavering as a serpentine-tailed comet." He sighs and leans his head into his hands for solace.

"I know it's Ramadan," Fred says, patting Abdul on the shoulder. "And that you haven't eaten, but don't be so gloomy. We're not all bad." Abdul pushes his wire rim glasses up on his nose, and his eyes look magnified through the lenses, his eyelashes long and his eyes wide.

"Fasting seven days makes one week. Or is that weak?" he says. His lips and face look pinched and pale under the olive skin.

"My mom came unhinged once," Maya says suddenly, uncharacteristically serious. "She thought she saw a man hiding in the attic, and swore he would kill us all. When my uncle went up to check it out, they found no one there. Can you imagine that? Seeing something that really isn't there?" She sighs and sits back against the red and gray nylon seat cover and absent-mindedly dusts off the armrest. A cop taps on the window, and Fred gets out of the car again.

"No, no damage," he says. The COSMOS truck driver hunkers down in his truck to avoid being lynched by the irate crowd – all victims of his momentary focus on the walking man. "Can I go now?" Fred asks. The cop shakes his head.

"Not yet."

A general confusion reigns until the cops get the victims to dig out their insurance forms and begin to fill them out. "Okay, you fill out one form with the car in front, and do another one with the car behind you. And mention the COSMOS man. The insurance companies will work it all out," the policeman reassures them. So little groups collect and huddle over crinkled hoods or trunks filling out forms, checking drivers' licenses, and getting to know intimate details of strangers.

"I can't believe I have to do this too," Fred protests. "Why can't we just go?" he moans to the cop.

"It's the rules," the policeman barks with his hands on his hips. Fred realizes that this "police man" is really a hefty woman with thick arms and shoulders, and hair cut into a bur like a prickly cactus. Her breasts hide, camouflaged under the tight uniform in a mass of muscled flesh. Fred's knees quake, and he almost salutes her. His heart fills with dread and a deep respect for the size and nature of things. He finally takes a deep breath and remembers himself once again, that he is on his way to work, and this is just a temporary obstacle on the path. Fred takes a pen from his khaki pants and obediently fills out the forms. Maya stands at his elbow cracking gum, and Abdul gets back into the car.

"What a mess," says the man whose car was hit by Fred's. He fills out the insurance form with Fred. "You see that naked guy running away from home?" He scratches his head and hands Fred his copy of the insurance paper. "I can relate to him," the man confesses. "Sometimes I want to do that too. Just leave it all behind, you know? I mean get up. Go to work. Come home. Same old, same old, day after day. What's the point of it all anyway?"

Fred shrugs. "Have a good day," he mumbles and waves Maya back into the car, fleeing the man with the existential crisis. The walking man now fiddles with the latches on his brief case. With the flip of a thumb, and then another, the thick brown case flies open and bills explode out in the wind. Euros fly across the ground, into the trees, and across the highway.

"Go for it!" Fred yells. Tires screech around them, doors fly open and people bound out, darting right and left to grab the bank notes.

Abdul leaps out of the car and chases the money as the wind bandies it about. Scores of people grab and push and grasp. They dodge open car doors, shove each other, and hurdle guardrails like Olympic athletes. Cars stop dead, angled in the center and on the shoulder of the road. Bills stick to windshields an instant before being torn away and lifted up again. People leap about in a chaotic dance, choreographed by the wind's invisible hand, which mocks anyone who thinks he's in control. Fred reaches and grabs and jumps. Maya scrounges and crawls under a bush. Abdul stands erect and serene, his hands clasped tight, a content expression on his face. The 50, 100, and 1000 Euro notes find their new homes in pockets, on roof tops, among the trash along the roadsides. People scrounge on hands and knees with their claws and nails in the shrubs and dirt, eager to collect what they can. The walking man keeps on going, oblivious to the excitement around him. Even the cops chase after the money instead of the naked man. When most of the Euros are collected or dispersed, Fred climbs in and starts the motor.

"Nothing," he laments. "I didn't get a single bill."

Abdul reaches for the car door and settles into his seat, patting his jacket pocket.

Maya hops in and perks up. "Look!" She squeals and waves a 100 Euro note between them.

"What about you?" Fred says. Abdul fondles his pocket, then crosses his arms. "How much did you get? A hundred?" Abdul pinches his lips together but remains silent. "More? Five hundred?" No response. "A thousand?" Fred insists; his voice raises an octave. Abdul freezes and looks away. "You found a thousand Euros! You lucky...! Why don't we split it?"

Abdul shifts uncomfortably. "We get what we deserve," he says. Fred looks glum and glides the car into gear.

"I didn't get a thing."

They pass the naked man. The two police officers, who have regained composure and purpose, now trail him on their motorbikes at a slow pace. The cops talk softly and try to cajole him into coming along quietly. The walking man seems not to notice. A Buddha-like smile spreads across his face. He seems to glow with an ethereal light.

"What are they going to do when they stop him? Let him ride naked behind one of 'em?" Abdul says. He shudders at the thought.

"They'll carry him nude through the streets like Lady Godiva," Maya says.

"I can't believe that," Fred says. "I used to have nightmares about being stuck at work naked, giving a presentation with nothing on." He shivers at the thought. "It was the creepiest thing. I felt awful. So vulnerable, you know?"

"You have hang ups," Maya asserts. "Naked bodies are beautiful."

"Oh, Allah," Abdul says. "There's a right place for everything. It should be kept in private."

"The Germans and Scandinavians don't think so," Maya insists. "I had a German boyfriend once…"

"Spare us the details." Abdul interrupts and crosses his arms. "What do you think happens to guys like that?" Abdul says pointing at the naked walking man out the window.

"I guess they'll put him in a psychiatric ward," Fred says.

"Just because he took off his clothes?" Maya says. "That seems unfair. Anyone should be able to take off their clothes when they want." She lifts her blouse and bares her breasts at the car beside them. The flower-print shirted tourists point and wave and the driver nearly veers off the road.

"What'er you doing?" Fred says. Abdul holds his head in his hands.

"She just bared her bosom. This is a holy time. It's Ramadan. Please respect my religious practices." Maya settles back into her seat and says nothing. Fred drives carefully, weaving back and forth between the left and right lanes, changing to keep a steady, even flow.

"*Mon dieu, mon dieu,*" Maya mutters silently, like it's a mantra. Fred speeds off down the pine-lined road toward the park entrance where the big computer companies sprout, take root, grow, and then move to India.

"I'm glad this week is almost over," Abdul sighs. "No more fasting next week."

"Good, you'll be back to your usual, well-adjusted, and happy self," Fred says patting him on the back. "And maybe you'll buy us lunch, since you're rich now."

"We have Lent," Maya spouts. "But I never give up anything. Why bother, I say."

"I do," Fred says.

"What?" Maya whines in disbelief.

"No chocolate, including chocolate croissants."

Abdul rolls his eyes.

"I live on those things. But once a year I stop for 40 days to take a break. It makes me appreciate it more later," Fred says. Maya scoffs.

"You should try it. It'll make you a better, stronger person," Abdul says to Maya.

"Oh look!" Maya cries out. "There's a man with a camel on a leash."

"See, I told you so," Fred says smugly.

"You're kidding. Makes me feel like I'm back in Algeria," Abdul groans.

"Some walk their dogs. But he takes his camel," Maya says. "I'd like a tiger. That would get some attention."

"It's a dromedary. They passed my apartment earlier," Fred insists, feels smug. The skeleton of a huge white and red tent begins to take shape in the empty field before the entrance to the park.

"So you're not seeing pink camels after all," Maya snorts.

The man walking the camel wears a red clown's nose and a sandwich board that reads Kara Boom Circus. Abdul looks relieved. Everything seems to be finding a new equilibrium after the crash and the camel, the naked man, and the serpentine comet, and the thousand Euro note nestled in his pocket. The hinges are on again. So the doors can close and open to let in just a little, just enough at a time. "I will tell the Imam that too," he thinks. He breathes a relaxed, even breath and reaches for the backpack at his feet.

"It's a three-day weekend you know," Maya says.

"Oh yeah," Fred perks up. "Thanks for the reminder. I would've come to pick you guys up on Monday. Just out of habit, you know? And because I love ya'." Fred pulls over at the curb and lets Maya and Abdul out. "See you guys later," he yells and waves. Abdul grunts and hurries off. Maya smiles and skips away, and Fred heads off to park and find his own cubicle while a man walking a camel on a leash holds up the morning traffic.

Chapter 3
The Flip Side of Life

Ian sat there staring out at the sea doing nothing for months. No more music in his head. No new words to write. It felt like being dead. But Trina stirred up an idea in him when she said, "You need more conflict. The easy life is making you dull." Trina talks like that, like she is a philosopher or something. *Sitting in a penthouse watching TV, you get soft. Too soft and everything looks far away, like looking through the wrong end of a telescope. I don't feel much anymore, mostly numb. But you'll think that's funny, a guy with my money and success, who owns so much stuff – that I feel empty. Ironic but true. So I made a decision. I let my beard grow all last week.*

The beard came out reddish and in patches, but his hair's brown. And he took some jeans worn bare in the knees and splotched them with coffee grounds and grease. Trina hasn't seen them yet, but she will. So this is what's going through his head this morning as he lays there. *Do I have the courage to wake up an icon and go out into the world a nobody?*

"Wake up, star," Trina says. She calls him star to mock him, he's sure. She is already dressed in a tight t-shirt and yoga shorts for her morning workout. Ian pulls the pillow over his head and feels the scratchy beard. "I wish you'd shave off that ugly thing. You don't look like yourself." She nudges him again. "Come on."

He can tell from her voice that she's fed up with him, with his boredom and depression. "Yeah, alright," he says. *I'm doing this for you, for us, for my music.* He feels hungry. *Last meal before I'm out on the street*, he thinks.

He groans. "I'd like three eggs this morning."

"Bad for your cholesterol," Trina says from the kitchen. He hears her voice from down the hall. "He wants three eggs, Sonia. Someday he's going to get fat," she tells the cook. The coffee aroma tickles his nose, and he puts on the grimy jeans and stained t-shirt. Trina hums an Indian tune she played on her reed flute last night and waits for him at the table. He sits down. The cook puts the croissants and eggs in front of him. "Gross! You're not sitting on the chairs dressed in that! You're going too far Ian. You're over the edge. You can't go anywhere in Monaco like that." Trina grabs a towel and throws it under him before he sits. "You see how he looks, Sonia!" The cook blinks and backs away.

"You think they'll kick *me* out? One of their glitterati," Ian says with a snort.

Trina's eyes twitch and her nose turns up in disgust. "I swear, if you weren't ..." She stops herself in midsentence.

"What? Go on. If I weren't rich? If I weren't famous? If I weren't handsome? Then they'd jail me? Then you'd leave me? Then I'd be happy?" She chews her croissant and egg like a horse, teeth grinding together and moving sideways. She sucks in some air.

"I wish you'd get yourself together."

"Well maybe that's what I'm doing," Ian says. Trina sips fresh orange juice.

"You have a plan?" Some hope stirs in her voice. He swallows some coffee.

"Exactly. Now, if you'll excuse me." He lifts the white linen napkin from his grimy jeans and places it beside the plate. Disappearing into the bathroom, he sees a stranger in the mirror. A bearded man with stringy shoulder-length hair and small dark eyes stares back at him. He pictures himself the way the magazines show him – always handsome, made-up, smiling. If only they could see him now. If only they could see the flip side. He squeezes the flat toothpaste tube from the bottom up and it squirts out a measly centimeter of white paste. *I'm flat like that toothpaste tube with nothing else to give. They squeezed me too much.* He brushes his teeth and appreciates that later today it might not be possible. He flosses too. He doesn't know how long this experiment will last. How long before life flows back into him and he feels alive.

On the bedside table, he only picks up cash and change. No credit cards or I.D. or anything else except his one lone house key that opens the lobby and his front door. But he spurns the bottle of antidepressants. Maybe it's better to ride the waves of despair and depression rather than be artificially even and numb. She watches him carefully. He can almost hear her thinking, *"He's lost it."*

"Going somewhere?" she says, her voice soft and pliable now.

"Out," he says. "I don't know when I'm coming back."

"Oh." Silence. Her brow wrinkles. "Are you taking your phone?"

"No, I don't think so. But I'll call later – if I can." And then he turns to face the door.

"Where are you going?" She refuses to kiss him. The beard tickles her, she complains. So he waves from the threshold. "I've got to go find…something."

***

In Monaco, the three mile by one-half mile country with video cameras and white-gloved police on every corner, he's the dirtiest thing on the street. Not a single piece of trash or a single beggar litter the sidewalk. It's clean, all clean on top. All dirty underneath. Dirty money flows into casinos and banks some say and is pumped out into legitimate investments. It's a tax haven too, where property prices equal downtown Manhattan or Paris. It's trying to become legitimate, this little country, by putting on a show, by appearing perfect and clean and safe.

It's early on a Saturday, May 15th, just a week before the Grand Prix, and the barriers and bleachers are going up. Ian partly lied when he said he had a plan. He only knew he would walk out the door, but doesn't know where he's going. Though he's lived here on the Mediterranean coast for a few years now, he's stayed mostly locked inside the apartment, mostly watching TV, mostly letting the world go by without him, despite calls of journalists and reporters who demand interviews and news about a next album. His shoulders slump. He drags his body along as if it were some cheap piece of luggage that he doesn't care much about. Even the contents don't seem to have much value to him. So he shuffles to the white marble station, white and pure and clean like new snow, and steps into the first train that arrives heading North without buying a ticket. Stations click past: Bealieu, Villefranche, Nice. Nice looks dirty too, like him, and big enough to be anonymous. The station's a dirty-pigeon grey filled with tourists, beggars, and some undercover cops who search a North African woman's bags for drugs. Trash bins overflow and it looks like the place hasn't been swept in years. It's a refreshing break from the phony life in Monte Carlo where they pretend it's all clean by making it clean on top, while underneath business men and celebrities evade taxes.

He steps out as the doors slide shut and he watches the cops and the unflinching face of the woman. "Did she swallow it?" one cop says. He snaps on surgical gloves and digs through her faded plaid suitcase. "I know she had it. I saw her take it from him." Ian's gut wrenches for her. He watches her expressionless face and thinks how her nerves must be of steel, on the outside at least. He continues down the stairs, underground, under the train tracks, and up again until he's finally out the door on the front steps of the station. Beggars with puppies hang out here. Drunkards plead for a few centimes for money for food they say, but they really want it for wine. Snot-nosed gypsy kids (Trina says he's supposed to call them *"gens de voyage"*, "transients" now, not gypsies) try to sell roses to tourists. They're dirty too, like the city. The streets are littered with "Le Big" wrappers, France's cheap fast food knock-off of McDonalds. What do you do in May here? It's starting to get hot at midday, but the sea breeze cools the air. It's the time of year when sunburns sneak up and leave you wretched and itchy at nightfall.

The shop windows filled with gold and diamonds, whole hams and sausages, Italian jeans and shoes flow past in nauseating waves down Avenue Jean Medecin. Once those things called out to him, beckoned, and he responded with yearning and desire. He had wanted to possess everything. But today, he feels unusually liberated of desire from things. Maybe lack of desire promises liberation, or merging, or some spiritual experience. People veer around him, step away. And this makes him laugh inside thinking of the irony of it all, how if they knew who he was behind the beard and the dirty clothes they'd be throwing themselves at him and begging for autographs instead. He chuckles a little out loud. A woman in front of him walks faster. *Maybe she thinks I'm dangerous.*

Where's there to go when you've already been everywhere? All the tours, the hotels, the cities, the press. What's left to see when you've already seen everything? Drugs, sex, violence, pornography. An old woman dressed entirely in black hobbles down the street using a cane to prop up her shaky figure. Her head is covered with a thick, black veil and she holds out a trembling metal cup. "Poor old woman," a voice behind him sighs and throws a ten Euro note into the cup. Other pedestrians contribute small coins to assuage their guilt at being healthy, fit, and youthful. Ian searches for the wad of bills in his pocket and gives her some. The figure trembles and hobbles along unmindful of the crowds, and he wants to tell the rushing pedestrians to be careful, that they might knock her over. But the people part like waves as she moves along slowly. When she turns down a side street, he follows her a little ways feeling like her guardian angel. He walks close behind to pick her up if she falls or to escort her back to her house if she has one. He imagines she must be lonely and desperate too. She turns and disappears into a darkened hallway, and he remains just out of sight in the shadows. Ian's eyes adjust as he follows her. The woman miraculously straightens. She leans the cane against the wall, pulls away her black veil, and instead of an old woman, a young one stands there counting her money.

"Hey wait a minute! You're not eighty!" Ian says indignant. He clasps her elbow. "I want my money back." She hides the cup under the folds of her long sleeves and rolls her lips back in a half smile, half snarl displaying a gap between teeth and brown lips.

"You paid for the performance. It's like any other show. We don't give refunds." Her voice is gruff like sandpaper. Her dark, gypsy eyes flash.

His compassion dies away, turns to shock and anger at her deception. "But...I gave money to a struggling old woman."

"Bah, it's a small price to pay for helping you to open your heart!" She tries to slip past, but Ian bars the way, planting his hands firmly into the walls on either side of the hallway. For the first time in months his passions stir. The numbing shell of dull comfort cracks away. She studies his face, stares directly into his eyes, and searches out the shapes of his cheek bones under the beard. A flicker of recognition races through her eyes. "You look a lot like that McKinesy guy," she says suspiciously.

He drops his hands from the wall. "Hmm. You think he would be out dressed like this?"

She pokes her head behind him and grabs his thigh. "Armani jeans?"

"Used."

"I read he lives near here. Bailed out here. Maybe he puts on disguises too. He needed an injection of life perhaps?" she says with a sly smile. He drops his hands and walks away feeling cheated, disillusioned, and found out. *People! Life would be fine without people.* A knee-high poodle on the sidewalk bounds up and sniffs at his knees. It wags its tail, happy to see him. He pets it, and its owner, a stooped old man, calls it back. *Dogs are friendly. Dogs make the French bearable.* Owners with their different breeds greet each other and compare notes on dog foods, vets, and doggie salons. Ian observes the dance from his park bench. Labradors sniff at Dachshunds; Boxers wag bobbed tails and nudge spaniels. When noontime draws around he starts to feel hungry. *Time to find a place for lunch.* The change in his pocket feels good now as he thinks of what he'll buy for lunch. A young woman, pretty, early twenties settles in beside him on the park bench leaving an empty space between them. Out of her plastic bag comes a baguette that she skillfully cuts down the middle, revealing its tender, white insides. On it she spreads thick slabs of butter and camembert. He looks longingly at the food. The hunger starts to gnaw at him. How rarely he feels hunger these days, he thinks. His belly is always full. He snacks all the time. But hunger enlivens him, provokes his brain cells to return to primordial necessities, to the will to live and survive.

She lifts the long baguette to her glossy pink lips, opens her mouth then snaps it shut without biting. "Would you stop staring at me, *s'il vous plait!*" Her exasperated voice sounds like a song.

"I'm sorry, I didn't realize I was staring like that. It was the bread, I was staring at. Not you." He laughs at himself, lusting after good French bread. "Not that you're not pretty. You are." She rolls her eyes then cuts the baguette in half.

"Here. Take that." She hands him half, and bites into the sandwich with a clear conscience, holding the other half out to him.

"No, really. I shouldn't," he says. "I'm on my way to get something."

Her eyes peer into him. "Your eyes say 'yes.'" She shakes it at him and continues with her mouth full. "Here. Take it."

"Thanks." The fresh bread, still warm from the oven, tastes sublime. It's the best he's eaten in a long time.

"Take some camembert if you want." The small round box of cheese sits on the bench between them.

"No thanks, really." Ian wrinkles his eyebrows, confused, and bites into the chewy bread. "Why'd you share?"

She stops chewing, peers into his face. "I feed stray dogs too. I bet you'd do the same."

"Yeah, I guess."

She hums one of his songs and he feels proud, excited. "That's mine," he blurts and points his finger at her.

"Don't exaggerate. This half is mine," she says.

"No. I mean the song."

"I can't get it out of my head. You like it too? You and a few million other people."

He wants to tell her he wrote it, that it came to him on a rainy day shortly after his brother died. Ian had considered putting a bullet into his own brain then. But looking at his dirty shirt and unkempt beard now, who would believe him? "It's so sad. I wonder where it came from," she says.

"I think he was feeling suicidal," Ian volunteers.

"Oh yeah, the words make sense now. Wow, you've put some thought into it. Most people just don't bother to think, you know."

He eats the sandwich, ravenously taking big bites. He tastes the musty rind of the cheese and swallows with contentment. You think those songs make a difference to anybody?" he says.

"You know," she reflects looking up toward a palm tree. "Sometimes just knowing someone else feels the same is enough. You know what I mean?"

He nods.

She checks her watch. "Time to get back to work," she sighs. "Run, run, run."

"Thanks," he says. "I mean really. Thanks."

"Sure." She hums his tune and waves absent-mindedly.

***

The shade diminishes as the sun moves overhead. Motivated by his desire to protect his tender skin, he tries to find a cool place. Ian walks out of the park. He walks and walks until he climbs up the hill to a garden filled with flowers, and Cyprus trees, and eucalyptus. Some benches under the trees offer protection from the harsh sun, and he stretches out there with one arm under his head and the other over his eyes. Thick cumulus clouds drift above on a deep blue canvas of sky. They rise and grow and shift until the images become internal and fuse with his thoughts. Images of his past unfurl like a film. Accepting a Grammy award when he was stoned. The first time he met Trina at a party. Throwing stones at windows in an abandoned house when he was a kid. The carefree feeling, the certainty that it would all work out...

When he awakens with a chill, a drizzle has started to fall on his cheeks and the sun is gone. He shivers and feels the stiffness in his back from the hard wooden bench. *I want to go home.* He fingers the cash in his pocket and thinks of the way back to the train station. Hunger gnaws at him again. The fresh air and uncertainty must burn more calories, he thinks as he edges his way to the seaside. An Asian fast-food restaurant on the sidewalk displays its fare behind thick glass: chicken in curry sauce, spring rolls, dim sum. The server dips them onto plates as Ian chooses and slides his tray down the cafeteria railing to the cashier. "Twenty-three Euros." She looks away from him when she speaks. He hands her the cash out of his wad of bills and walks to a table to eat.

The spring rolls with shrimp are the best he's ever eaten. The tepid dim-sum dipped in red hot chili sauce makes his tongue tingle. His senses are aglow with the hot food and the electric neon light. Happily, he is a million miles away from the five star restaurants with stuffy waiters and foods so rich they make him sick. Immersed in his moment of joy, his eyes are sealed shut in delight. A man's voice interrupts. "I saw that wad. Where'd a bum like you get that kind of cash?" The fellow is burly with thick hair on his neck and arms.

"I earned it."

"Yeah, sure. And I'm the Queen of England."

"A queen, maybe," Ian mutters.

The man throws his paper towel on the orange tray and leaves.

Ian savors each dish, filling his belly with contentment. *Simple things make life good.* This is what he discovers, what he notes in his new philosophies on life.

***

On the street, Ian hums the tune the girl hummed at lunch, one of his favorites too. The hairy man from the restaurant steps up from

behind and hooks his arm under Ian's. Another man approaches
and holds his other arm. Together the men pull him into a side
street. "Who's the queen?" the big man growls. He empties Ian's
pockets, takes the cash, and throws the key on the ground then
slams Ian across the back of the neck with his thick forearm.
Down on the pavement, Ian grabs the key and watches their boots
disappear. *I'm ready to go home.* He hobbles back to the train station,
head aching, shoulders bruised. This time he has no money for a
ticket and hopes that no controllers work the late shift. *You can
usually count on the French to slack off on the job, especially at night. so
it should be a cinch*, he thinks.

As the train pulls out, he sits on the pull-down seat by the door
and the lights flicker past. Light – dark. Light – dark. The train
picks up speed and a rhythm sets in. Th-thump. Th-thump. Th-
thump. Th-thump. The rhythm enters his bones and he brings it
together with the sound of a wailing baby a few seats behind him.
Aaoowwheee! Lost identiteee. He snaps his fingers in rhythm with
the wheels on the track. A moment of meditation, of dislocation,
of reconnection. *Lost identity,* he hums out loud. *Retrieving my lost
identity. Going back to my home by the sea. Where my baby's waiting for
me.* The train halts. The doors slide back with a heave like they'll
probably go on strike soon. A uniformed woman steps in, looks
down at him, and the doors slam shut again. "Tickets," she announces. A couple of teenagers walk to the back and disappear
through the doors. The train slides out of the station. Ian pulls the
white insides of his pockets out to show he has nothing. "Where's
your ticket?" Ian looks into her round face. His mom looked like
that, dull, permed hair, and splotched cheeks. She takes out a pad
and writes him a ticket.

"Your name?"

"Huh?"

"What's your name? *Vous parlez français*?"Before he went on stage they called him Woody. Even his mom picked it up because he was so hard-headed, hard like wood – always wanting his own way.

"Woody."

"Woody what?" He looks around and the train pulls into another stop.

"Woody Warbler," he says with a deadpan face. The woman rolls her eyes. The song flows through his mind. *I'm paying my dues to society.* The train screeches to a halt at a tiny station that seems to be in the middle of nowhere.

"This is your stop, Woody," the woman announces. *It's the price to pay for anonymity.* He stuffs his hands in his pockets and mumbles.

"I got two million in the bank." She tears off the ticket and shoves it in his face. When the train stops, she waits and watches him step out onto the darkened platform. He shuffles along, feet heavy now. His longing to get home grows stronger with each step and so does the music in his head. *Aaooowwhee! Lost identity.* He sits down on a dew-dampened bench and stares at the moths flickering around the street lights. *Another train'll come by soon. Maybe in an hour or two or maybe in the morning.* The words and tune to the song, his new song play through his head. *The music's back! It's back!* But there's no paper. So he starts to write in the dust of the flowerbed by the tracks to capture the words and the melody. Joy and relief sweep through him. There's something serene in the silence and the solitude of the deserted station. He feels like a lone traveler on an itinerary mapped out just for him and he feels the magic of life. For an instant he recalls the face of a Buddhist Monk he once met. The man looked still inside, as if he had all the answers and nothing perturbed him. *That's the way I want to be. Peaceful and filled with serenity. No more lost identity.*

Chapter 4

Peaking in Monaco

The mountain looks insurmountable. Nicholas Monet climbs. It does not matter that he is wearing his most expensive business suit and wing-tipped shoes. He puts one foot in front of the other and goes straight up the mountain. The higher he goes the steeper and more rugged the path becomes. It transforms from a walk over a rocky path into a climb straight up a sheer rocky cliff. Despite his slippery-soled shoes, he finds a steady foot hold, hooks the cord attached to his harness into a piton, and clips the metal latch there for safety. He reaches up. A stone ledge hangs over his head and he studies the surface and the ridges of the rock to find the best hold for his next move. At this height, he is alone. No one follows him. No one is near. He knows never to look back, never to look down, but for an instant, the moment when he is about to reach out for the next hold with his right hand, it strikes him. There is a long drop off below.

He can't afford to fall. He must keep going, struggling, striving, straining. His foot slips. A shower of rocks falls away from under him, and he hears a crack. Terror shoots through him. It's time to change, he thinks. He promises to change. He wants to change. He clenches the narrow finger-holds tighter, pushes up on his toes to make the next move. He moves up, but the whole slab of rock beneath him where the piton was anchored slips. Down. His stomach leaps up. He feels queasy. He clings tighter. The rock he clings to, the size of a house wall, splits away from the cliff. Falls. He flies through the air, the rock tied to him by a cord, chasing him. He hits. Jerks. Bounces up. Sits up in bed.

"Jeezus." Nick says. Sweat pearls on his forehead, soaks the bed sheets. He looks around and tries to remember. Monday, Sydney. Yesterday, London. Today (if you can call 12:45 a.m. day), Monaco. He is in his penthouse apartment with the terrace that plunges fifteen floors down to the sea. Thinking of the terrace makes him shudder. His guests, on the rare occasions that he had any, would look at him with envy and pity as they stood outdoors, and beckoned him to join them. But he would only stand inside, far behind the glass doors to enjoy the dizzying view and never venture out there.

***

Nick's Jaguar purrs. Even though it's June, he keeps the windows closed and the air conditioner on. Some people might prefer the cool sea breeze, but he likes to regulate the temperature at exactly 72 degrees Fahrenheit. A mass of white cumulus clouds hangs over the sea in the distance and reminds him of a recent postcard he received from his ex and his daughter. The air sparkles. The garden brims with sculptures by Bottero, royal palms, and gladiolas. He looks in the rear-view mirror, not to see what's behind, but to study his once handsome and youthful face. But the man he once knew and expected to see is not there. Another man stares back. He has creases at the corners of his eyes, dry skin, greying hair at the temples. A dark, brown mole grows on his chin and dark circles spread out under his eyes. Jetlag always makes him feel a century old. And he seems to be in a permanent state of jetlag now, always six hours ahead or nine hours behind. But never on time. His mind feels like a jar of rubber cement broke inside of it, and the thoughts that rise are sticky, and long, and drawn out just like his reactions. Sooner or later he will catch up with himself, he thinks. Then he'll be alright again, like new, like when he was thirty and ready for anything.

His car drives down the road past the garden, past the stop light when she pulls out in front of him and he slams on the brakes. BANG. Her old, yellow Karmann-Ghia ends up with the nose of his Jag in its back fender. Her car has a French license plate, not Monegasque like his. He throws his hands in the air. Curses. Gets out of the car. The woman opens her door and stands up. She's like an amazon with broad shoulders and a kind, friendly face. She could even be pretty if she wore some makeup and changed out of those khaki hiking shorts, he thinks.

"You know you ran through the light?" she says, unruffled. "It was green for me, which means it was red for you." He looks at her, thinks back to his thoughts when he drove through and realizes he was on automatic pilot and remembers nothing. She looks up at the Monaco street camera that would have recorded the scene.

"Oh. Seemed like it was red to me," he says feebly, too tired to argue or bully her.

She examines the damage and runs her strong fingers over the fender. "It's hard to get parts for her. I hope she can be repaired without too much trouble."

Nick crosses his arms over his chest in anticipation of a verbal assault, accusations, rage and name-calling. But when he sees her composed face, he uncrosses his arms and studies her more closely. She pulls an accident form out of the glove compartment and begins to fill out her half.

"I guess you've got good insurance, huh?" she says.

"I guess. My secretary takes care of it." Nick watches her fill out her name – Sandra –her address – Villefranche. She begins to draw the little diagram that the insurance companies will use to determine who is at fault. Someone must always be at fault, he thinks.

"What's the name of this street?" she says and looks around for the signs. He shrugs. "Don't spend much time here, do you?"

"No. I'd like to. But with the business and all." Nick admires the well-defined muscles of her arms and sees the straps of the sports bra showing from under her tank top. Longing washes over him like a tidal wave, leaving an empty shore of loneliness in its wake. How long's it been? He thinks back to the divorce, the slew of women from hotel bars on business trips, and finally the worn out, deflated feeling the days after. Maybe it is time to settle down, find a solid, good-hearted woman who loves him for himself.

The woman's sandy colored ponytail brushes against the bare part of her back where the neck of her tank makes a U. He would like to reach out and touch her, though he has not been prone to acts of affection or had any need for it (so he often tried to convince himself) for some time. Making money and business were his *raison d'etre*. Isn't that enough for anyone? She hands him the pen and he notices the lack of rings on her fingers.

"You want to fill out your part?" she says.

"Sure. But my information is confidential."

"What? You think I'd sell it to a mail order company? Now there's an idea," she says a little sarcastically.

He leans the paper against the hood of her car and begins to fill in the blanks, while Sandra leans back, one leg crossed at the ankle, her arms crossed over her chest. "You have a boyfriend?"

"Huh?"

"You seeing someone?" She looks at him sideways.

"Aren't you too old for me?"

He feels embarrassed, remembers his worn face in the mirror. "I don't think so."

"You wouldn't," she says. He glances at her birth date and calculates she is twenty-eight.

"How old do you think I am?" he says. He finishes writing on the form.

She takes it from him, looks over it to make sure it's complete, then tears out one of the copies for him. "This is yours."

"So, how old do you think I am?" he repeats.

She takes a deep breath and sizes him up. "Probably old enough to be my father."

"Yes, if I would have started at age twelve. Come on, I don't look so old. I'm only 38," he says. "Go out to dinner with me tonight."

"What?"

"I'd like to take you to dinner."

"But…"

"Come on. Just once. Then if you don't like me… And if I don't like you, we don't have to see each other again."

She folds the document and tosses it on the front seat of the car. "Well, I suppose it's like gambling," she says, looking over at the ornate façade of the casino. "If you never take a risk, you never have a chance of winning the jackpot."

"Great," he says, feeling like he's just signed a new contract. He looks at his copy of the accident form and feels suddenly buoyed up. "Shall I pick you up here at this address?"

"Why don't we meet at the Café de Paris by the casino over there and start with a drink?" she says.

"Say six o'clock?"

"Sounds fine to me..uh," She quickly picks up the paper on the seat and reads his name. "Nick."

"Good. See you later, Sandra."

***

When Nick arrives at the Café, Sandra stands on the sidewalk in front of the tables waiting for him, a huge smile on her face. She wears Lycra stretch shorts and a sports bra with her bare, muscular stomach showing.

"That's pretty informal for the place I want to take you," he says. She eyes him up and down.

"That will not do," she says. He wears a linen jacket with a black polo shirt, thin summer cotton pants, and slick-soled Church's shoes that passed at board meetings and impressed clients, but did not please Sandra.

"They're fine for dinner."

"Not where we're going." Sandra holds up a backpack and winks at him. "I brought dinner, but we've got a little work to do before we can eat."

Nick worries as he stares into her open, guileless face. "I'm kinda tired from jetlag. What exactly did you have in mind?"

Her eyes flash with enthusiasm and she points up to the cliff above them. "We're going up there. I was on my way earlier when you hit me, so I had to postpone. It's the best view of the entire coast."

Her biceps are taut and well-defined. Her thighs and calves are muscular. She doesn't have an ounce of fat on her body.

"You're kidding, right? Besides it'll get dark."

She shakes her head no. "Not today. It's the solstice. The longest day of the year. And later we'll have the full moon too. There'll be plenty of light."

"I don't know. It's not like I had planned." They face each other and she rocks her shoulders back and forth in a comfortable rhythm almost like a child.

"It'll do you good. As my grandma used to say, 'nothing clears your head like a whiff of cool mountain air.'"

He sighs. His muscles still ache from the twelve hour flight, but he wants to be alone with her. Some of her youthfulness might seep into him, renew him, inspire him, even give him a new sense of purpose. "Well, okay," he says. "But I need to change shoes and put on some shorts."

"Great," she says. "I'm going to take my car too. We'll go to your place first. Then you can follow me."

"Why can't we take one car and go together?"

"It'll give us more independence this way," Sandra says. "I like to be able to come and go as I want." This is usually his line. He wants to protest, but she is already a step ahead of him, walking toward the entrance to the parking garage. He skips a step to catch up with her.

***

Nick follows Sandra up the curving, narrow road with the steep drop off. His stomach feels queasy without any dinner and his head aches from the concentration. He wishes she would go slower. The full moon rises over the sea like a huge disk of opal. But he dares not look at it for more than half a second for fear of missing the next hair-pin curve and following in the footsteps of Princess Grace, who plunged toward tiny Monaco below, and ended up on the rocks. They reach a narrow pull off where they park the cars. Nick feels his stomach churn with acid and the bitter taste of the malt whiskey he drank earlier burns his throat. He slides his car next to Sandra's, opens the door, and holds his head out looking down the cliff. The damp evening coolness surrounds him and sends a chill up his back. The hair on his arms stands on end. Sandra jumps out of her car and throws some thick blue ropes over her shoulder then tosses him a harness.

"What's that for?"

"I told you we had to do some work to get to the place. The reward's the view."

He sizes up the ropes and a glimmer of understanding begins to inch into his brain. It was supposed to be a quiet dinner in a restaurant with an attractive (albeit Amazon-like) woman, to soothe his loneliness. He had toyed with the idea that he might even bring her home. He had not planned to be outdoors about to scale a cliff, about to die. His palms sweat. Maybe he should go home now to a hot dinner in the pub on the corner and then return safely to his crisp cotton sheets. Of course, he would avoid the apartment terrace with its steep drop off and its fantastic view of the summer moon. He might slip. It was always a possibility. But then again, there was the railing. But still he likes to play it safe and stay inside, far behind the doors.

"Listen," he says looking around. Several cars, mostly ten or twelve years old – models of Fords, Golfs, Fiats – sit up and down the roadside. He looks at Sandra full of energy and life. His own face, he knows, is drawn and tense and he wants to run away. But something in her smile, the sparkle in her eyes – and especially his fear of being called a coward, urges him on and he takes the harness and falls in step behind her, not wanting to disappoint. His polo shirt, heavy with sweat, clings to his chest. His legs tremble.

They walk along a narrow path, past a small, stone animal shelter where goats bleat. Their musky stench fills the air and Nick sneezes. A billy goat blocks the path and Sandra pushes its hind end to move it away, and walks on. But when Nick steps up beside it, the goat stares at him with slit pupils that look like a devil's and butts him with its horns. Sandra turns and laughs at the sight of Nick fearfully scurrying away from the animal. They edge around a bend, then the sea appears in view. The stone cliff rises up at their backs like a formidable fortress wall.

Some people cling to the cliff above them. Sandra looks up and waves. "Hey, guys," she says. "Perfect night for a climb." Other guys and one or two young girls stand below them, staring up. They all seem young as adolescents, but Nick realizes it is his own feeling of growing old and tired that makes them look so young. They must be in their twenties. All of them look lean and athletic wearing their spandex shorts and thin-soled climbing shoes. He reaches out and touches his paunch, then sucks it in self-consciously under his expensive polo shirt. He again longs to go back to the luxury and comfort of his apartment. How nice it would be to step into the hot Jacuzzi and let the jets of water pound against his loose flesh and tight neck muscles. Nick clenches and unclenches his jaw and fists.

"Here, we'll do this one," Sandra says. "See that ledge up there?" She points to a place about 50 meters up the rock wall. "That's where we'll stop and have dinner."

Nick sizes it up. The stone wall in front of him holds pitons, and a path straight up is more or less visible with possible holds for a foot or a hand every meter or so. "Listen, why don't you go? I'll watch. Then we can go for dinner. That'll be enough for me."

"This is an easy climb. You never climbed before?"

He stops. Thinks. Wants to tell her that he climbs in his sleep every night, and that he always falls. Never makes it to the top.

"This is just a short one. Doesn't require you to be in top shape." She reaches out and grabs his biceps to size them up. "You'll do fine." She slips her legs into the harness, and tightens it over her shoulders. She motions for him to do the same. He pulls up his harness, but fumbles with the plastic buckles. Sandra closes them for him and tightens the straps around his chest. Her fingers look thick and strong, and a little rough. A long way from the finely manicured and polished women from the escort service that he takes to dinner when clients bring wives and when he needs late night company. Paid company. Friendship for a price. He wonders why he asked Sandra to dinner. Desperation? Loneliness? He could have just called the agency again or gone home alone. Funny how she didn't seem to care about his car or his clothes, but kept staring into his eyes like she was trying to decipher the secrets of his heart and find out what was really inside. If only he knew he might share it with her, since he probably will never see her again anyway.

"Have you ever been in love with anyone?" he says. Her back is turned and she faces the cliff looking up at the first piton.

"What?"

"Love. Have you ever loved anyone?" He thinks that he probably hasn't loved anyone before. Not his first wife. Not his kid who he never sees. And possibly not even himself. But Sandra with her strong back and big shoulders, her way of standing straight and solid, Sandra must certainly know about love. She must surely love herself. Sandra turns her head to look over her shoulder.

"Why do you want to know?" She turns back to the rock, reaches up and grasps a narrow ledge, then pulls herself up. She latches the metal clip through the first piton and puts her cord through it. "There." Her right foot edges into a narrow slit in the rock and she lifts her body up another 12 centimeters and, steadying herself, she looks around for the next hold for her left hand. She looks like a spider stretched out against the rock wall, inching her way up from one narrow hold to another. She turns to look down at him. "You can start."

"But…" He doesn't want to and he considers dropping the harness and walking away. But he remembers how good he felt once when he faced his fear. At the age of twenty, he stood up to his father and said he would not go to university to study business. He risked being despised and rejected, but he decided it was more important to him to have the courage to follow his heart. And he did it. He went to Africa instead, just like his Uncle James had done. His father turned his back and never sent him another check. Nick had saved face with himself, but he ended up with a tropical worm in his intestines that made him perpetually hungry. The doctors said he would never be one-hundred percent free of it.

So he came back physically debilitated, and literally paid for his choice by working his way through the rest of school. The irony came when he graduated and accepted a job with a big company to pay off his loans. So he ended up in business despite his initial choice of adventure, and a parasite that made him perpetually hungry. Maybe after that he didn't put much stock in following his heart, and most of the time he couldn't even hear what it was saying to him anyway. He watches Sandra move easily from one piton to another. It looks easy, almost as easy as climbing stairs. Some young men stand a few feet away watching her while one of their buddies rappels down the cliff from 120 meters above.

"Come on," she beckons Nick. The guys look at him and he looks back at them, then up at Sandra. They seem to smirk at his polo shirt and new, white jogging sports shoes. His fear of ridicule or of being called a coward over-powers his fear of climbing. He looks for a solid hold for his right hand and reaches up to the rock. He inches up, holds on, and pulls himself up a little higher. His foot slips and he scratches his chin. The guys snicker. But he holds on, grabs a narrow ledge and pulls himself up again. His legs and arms strain under his weight. Then with a rush of adrenaline, a feeling of determination kicks in and he raises himself up to the second piton and onto the third. Sandra perches above him and leans back with her legs straight out against the cliff. "You're almost there," she says, looking down with a smile. Nick imagines the faces of the guys standing below them, wondering what she sees in him. On the evolutionary scale, he probably could not compete with them. They look younger, tougher, and probably have more vitality. But he has money, maturity, and charm. Maybe she would go home with him after all, after his super-human effort to climb the mountain for her. For most women the other stuff was enough: a dinner, a nice car, a little talk. But he wants to prove himself to Sandra.

Nick loosens up and concentrates one-hundred percent on his movement. He transfers his weight and his balance. With the concentration, the hint of fear that threatened to overwhelm him remains out of bounds, out of sight. He follows Sandra's example and hooks the cord attached to his harness into the first metal clip. He tugs at the piton, testing its resistance. Satisfied that he is safe, he looks up for the next one. "I must be insane," he thinks out loud. But he does not look down and instead inches steadily upward. His shoes are not the best, not the totally flexible kind like Sandra and the other experienced climbers have, but she said his Nikes would do. And for some reason, he trusts her, maybe more than he has ever trusted anyone. It seems his life is in her hands. Maybe he trusts her because he senses that she does not want to take anything from him. Everybody else he knows wants something: money, contracts, contacts, a free meal. But this Sandra girl wouldn't even allow him to buy dinner. She brought it with her. He starts to feel hungry and wonders what she carries in her backpack. It certainly wouldn't be filet mignon with Béarnaise sauce. But that's okay, he could use something lighter. Eating less meat would help him lose weight. Sandra reaches the ledge and stands on the edge peering down at him.

"Hey, you almost made it." She encourages him and steps back out of sight. His arms feel the ache of overuse and he feels a little scared with Sandra out of view.

"You still there?" he says weakly. She steps back into view with a bowl in her hand and removes the plastic wrap.

"Yeah. I'm setting the table for your dinner." With another push, one hand is on the ledge and his legs push him up. He ends up on his belly and pulls his legs over the ledge too until all of the pieces of his body are there and he can sit up.

"There," he pants. "Made it. That had better be a good dinner," he warns her.

"The best." A blanket covered with a bowl of cherries, a plate of cheese and grapes, sliced baguette, thin slices of Prosciutto ham and Cavaillon melon and some plastic cups wait for him.

"You're kidding. It looks like a caterer came and set it up before we got here," he says. She even has a candle and a bottle of chilled rosé. "What do I owe you for this?"

"Is money all you think about?" She shakes her head and pulls the cork out of the wine bottle. "This is priceless. No noisy tables of people around. No snobby French maître d's. And look at the view!"

"Did you do all this just for me?"

"I was actually planning on coming on my own anyway. A little celebration of the solstice. It's my favorite day of the year. There's so much light today. I know it's only June, but after this the days get shorter, and I find that a little sad. I guess if I had the money, I'd follow the sun across the globe all year round. Have an endless summer, you know?" Nick accepts a plastic cup of wine from her and looks at her face again. Out here in nature, she looks like a child with the glow of the rising moon striking her face and softening her features. Nick leans over the edge and looks down at the drop-off below them. The worst will be getting down, he thinks. It's always harder to make it back down after being so far above others. Sandra reaches over to unfasten his harness. He brushes her hands away.

"No. I'll leave it on."

"Suit yourself." She lifts her glass in the air to toast him, then takes a drink and begins to eat a piece of cheese with the baguette.

"Ever fall?" he says.

"All the time. I fell out of trees, off of my mom's roof top, down a crevasse once. I hate it. But I always get back up and keep going." He looks at her, his eyes intent, his brows crease his forehead with worry lines. "Never been seriously hurt though. I think climbing must be in my genes. Since I was a kid, I always wanted to climb to the top of anything." She reflects and watches him eat a grape. "I bet you're kind of the same. You're a climber. Only you don't usually scale mountains."

"Yeah, I guess." He feels proud of himself.

"My dad. He was just like you. Nothing ever mattered except getting to the top. It was like a sickness to him. If the neighbors bought a new car, he'd go out and buy a bigger, more expensive one. He couldn't be happy for other people's good fortunes."

"Well, I'm not exactly like that." Nick thinks back to his brother who bought a new house in the Caymans recently and feels a little guilty. Nick had bought the bigger house next to it and let his brother know how much he'd paid. Now they would be neighbors, though Nick didn't have the intention of going there when his fat brother and chatty wife were around.

"Can I ask you something?" she says. He leans on one elbow and begins to feel like a Roman emperor at the height of his reign. But he does not say anything. He only looks back at her satisfied with the view, her light company, and the moon for as long as he does not think of the height and the ledge. "Why did you ask me out?"

"Why did you accept?" he says.

"I figured you were just here on business and lonely."

"I could have called an escort."

She turns up her nose as if his words have a bad odor. "You do that kind of thing?"

He says nothing. "May I have some more wine please?"

"Careful, it's like truth serum. Soon you'll be revealing all of your deep, dark secrets," she laughs.

"And fantasies," he adds, then feels embarrassed. A sense of freedom fills him. He is liberated from himself – temporarily – from the roles, the social conventions, the fear of faux pas, and the great effort of making conversation so that people will like him. "Do you think I'm likeable?" He knows that Sandra owes him nothing. She is free to say what she wants and does not depend on him to buy her dinner or even to drive her home. In this way, he is pretty sure that he will get an honest answer.

"I was just thinking about that."

"So?"

"No, not really. I mean, I think you could be. If you would loosen up. You're so stiff, like you want to stay in control or something. If you'd be a little more spontaneous and let more of your real self come through…"

His real self. He hadn't been his real self probably since he was in high school. No maybe it was earlier, in grade school. Or maybe he never was his real self. He never dared to be. Never thought anyone would like that self, and so he pretended to be what pleased everyone else: his parents, his wife, his boss, the board.

"I'm sorry," Sandra says. "Sometimes it's better to pretend, I guess. But I'm not very good at it. People always see through me." Nick stares off into space, into his own thoughts. "Here, have some more wine," she says.

"Trying to get me drunk? Then I won't be able to climb down."

"Oh, we're not going down," she says and smiles at him the

serene smile of the Mona Lisa. "We're only going up."

Nick chokes on the grape in his mouth. He coughs and coughs. Sandra strikes him on the back to dislodge it. "What do you mean we're only going up? It looks like there's at least a hundred more meters above us."

"That's a pretty accurate estimate. Eat up so you'll have enough energy to get to the top."

Nick rolls his eyes. Is this a bad dream he has fallen into? Maybe he will awaken soon and find himself in his own bed, sitting up saying "Jeezuz" because he has just fallen. Maybe it is all just a dream.

Chapter 5
Degrees of Separation

"Your task is not to seek for love, but merely to seek and find all the barriers within yourself that you have built against it," the actor says on bended knee. The blue velvet curtain falls. The audience applauds in a burst of joy. Vicki D'Angelo clasps her handbag, sighs heavily, and stands up to file out of the theatre behind the happy crowd.

"How beautiful," Cara whispers, as the tips of her fingers push Vicki from behind. "I love Rumi!"

"Yeah," Vicki says, but unconsciously shakes her head no.

"Rumi would have liked champagne," Cara says. "He had that bubbly feeling of love."

"Whatever," Vicki says.

"Don't tell me you didn't like it!" Cara says.

"Well… It's just not real. He may be a saint or a mystic or whatever, but you can never really know another's heart. It's just impossible," Vicki says with a slight frown fixed to her lips. Her shoulders are curled forward as they push out into the lobby.

"Whoa. What are you so down about?!"

The play about the Sufi mystic, Rumi, had hit Vicki in the heart. It talked of love and connection, but for a while now, an inkling, a notion had lingered just beneath the surface of her consciousness. Life is made of barriers and we're walled off from others, she thinks. At age twenty-five, Vicki feels numb and lonely. A huge abyss divides us, she thinks. We reach out but never really touch another and feel his pain or joy. How often do we speak without being heard and understood? Or we wear masks that make us strangers even to ourselves. They step outdoors into the chilly evening air and walk toward the Promenade des Anglais.

"The play got it wrong. There's only separation. Look at the Great Wall of China or the Berlin wall!" Vicki reflects, worries, and resigns herself to this reality. She walks staring at the sidewalk.

Cara stops and faces her. "The Berlin wall fell."

"They put up a new one in Israel to keep people out."

"It's for protection."

"That's what they all say."

"And almost anyone can walk on the Great Wall of China now."

"It's still a barrier," Vicki says.

Cara ponders and searches for an idea of infinite space. "They dropped the borders between most European countries," she says. "And look at the sea." She motions to the bay and the Mediterranean Sea in the darkness beyond them. "There are no walls around the sea."

"But there are coasts."

"Fortunately for us since we live on land!" Cara shakes her finger, exasperated. "You...you're thinking too much. Rumi wrote about a feeling. Something you have to experience and then you get it."

"Yeah, but it's not reality. We're all cut off from each other. It's just the way life is."

"You think of walls. I think of open space," Cara says. "You think no one understands you, but I know you better than I know my own sister." Their eyes meet, but Vicki quickly looks away. "It happens here to here," Cara says touching her own heart and then touching Vicki's. "Not here to here." Cara touches Vicki's forehead and then her own. "You need a hug!" Cara reaches out and warmly embraces her and Vicki limply responds. "Come on. I'll buy you a double *kir royale*. Bubbles always perk you up...Or they used to anyway before you turned all dreary."

"Sorry," Vicki says. She secretly feels like crying, but fights back the tears. Vicki thinks of the sea's infinite horizon and how the stories of limits changed. Navigators once imagined you'd drop off the edge of the earth if you sailed far enough. But now everyone knows that if you sail far enough, you only reach another shore, another boundary.

"Let's walk over to the flower market. It's livelier," Cara says.

Vicki pulls her light jacket around her shoulders, and Cara hooks her arm inside of Vicki's to keep in step. On the *Promenade* they look out over Angels' Bay. Waves crash against the stone walls below them where parasols and tourists stretch out in summertime. As the waves withdraw, fist-sized pebbles roll and churn, filling the air with a deafening roar. Another huge wave curls in from the darkened bay like a sea serpent rising up from the ocean floor. It breaks against the wall flinging spray on them like a heavy shower of rain.

"*Oh la la*," Cara cries out. "I got drenched!" Her hair drips with beads of salt water. "I probably look like a wet poodle." She clings to her raincoat. Vicki stares into the darkness. Her thoughts seem churned up and thrown about like the rocks on the shore. Another wave rises in the distance, gaining in power until its white foamy head becomes visible. Just as it is about crash, Cara grabs Vicki.

"Let's get out of here!"

Vicki lets herself be pulled away, but watches the waves over her shoulder. "I could watch the sea for hours and never get bored."

"No, but you might get drenched. Come on." Cara coaxes her away from the seafront and past a hotel with a sign in front – *International Psychic Fair*. "Let's stop here so I can dry off in the restroom. Didn't you get wet?"

"Not much. I'll wait for you." Vicki stands in the lobby, and Cara returns with a light step.

"Want to see the future?" she says. "The fair's free." Cara leads her into a big room set up with individual booths. A black curtain with silver stars and moons hangs over the front of one booth. An Asian man sporting a long ponytail sits at a table decorated by a Himalayan salt lamp and mandalas. Soothing music plays over the speakers.

"Who would you like to talk to?" Cara says.

"Who me? I don't do that kind of stuff. The future scares me."

"Oh come on." Cara nudges Vicki. "They're giving readings. How fun! I love these places." She places a finger beside her nose and scans the room. "I'm going to see her," she points to a woman dressed in bright blue. "I like her color. I hope she'll tell me about the man of my dreams."

"I'll wait for you over there," Vicki says, embarrassed at the idea she might hear something about Cara's life that she shouldn't know. She stands near the entrance, her arms crossed over her chest and she avoids eye contact with the clairvoyants in the booths. A woman with long black hair and fingernails painted black brushes her arm.

"Oh, excuse me," she says and turns to go. But she suddenly stops and turns back to observe Vicki. Vicki backs away, uncomfortable at the scrutiny. "You feel like no one has ever understood you," the woman says. She lays a finger at the center of her lips and seems lost in thought.

Vicki's eyebrows rise. "Yeah, how can anyone ever understand anyone else?" She blurts out. Tears form in her eyes.

"You'll see. Very soon you're going to have an experience that will change you." The woman touches her arm reassuringly. The touch sends an electrical current through Vicki's body. Then she disappears down an aisle.

Cara emerges from the booth with a wide smile just in time to notice the woman. "Was that someone you know?"

"Not at all."

"Well listen to this. She says there's a perfect man for me. I just knew it. I may meet him on a boat," she squeals. Vicki stands speechless and perplexed. "Is anything wrong?" Cara says. The crown of Vicki's head tingles and she scratches it.

"I'm ready for that drink you promised."

On the street they walk by the ocher and yellow facades of the 19th century buildings on the *Cours Salei*. In the open square, flower market stalls line the cobblestone street. Fish restaurants spread out on either side. Their ice-filled cases display sole, sea bass, snails, oysters, and spiny, black sea urchins. A sea bass struggles on the ice; its gills stretch open as it suffocates in the air. How ironic, Vicki thinks. This morning you were out there in the Mediterranean, and the sea is just a few meters away, but now you're cut off here, dying. She has a sudden urge to buy it and release it in the sea.

"You hungry?" Cara says watching her ponder the fish. "We could stop if you like." Vicki shakes her head.

"No."

"I love sea bass baked in rock salt and served up with rosé. Mmmm. But that's a summertime thing for me."

"Actually, I think I may become a vegetarian. I mean look at these poor guys," Vicki says. Cara rolls her eyes and drags Vicki along. Cafés decorate the far end of the wide, open piazza. Cara pulls out a metal seat at *"Les Trois Diables"* and Vicki sits down.

"I'll go order. Their service is lousy." She gets up to go to the bar and leaves Vicki alone in the crowd. Couples sit huddled together against the damp breeze holding hands, staring into each others' eyes. So close, she thinks, but nevertheless separate, isolated. She had sat here like that with Theo, her ex-boyfriend. He had lived in his own little world. He focused solely on painting and writing, and he ridiculed her doing secretarial work at the financial services company. He was hyper-sensitive and nervous like a high-strung horse. She had truly wanted to experience the way that Theo saw the world, what he felt. She loved his painting, but his brooding and moodiness kept her always a little out of reach. She had to keep up her armor of self-defense to protect herself. He would be a sweet and tender boy one day, and in an instant, shift into a harsh and critical ogre. It seemed as if he threw out criticism and hurtful words like knights once threw rocks and hot oil from the high walls of guarded castles. And so she built up solid walls too. It's natural isn't it? She wonders. For every action there is an equal and opposite reaction, scientists say. The principle works in relationships too. Every hurt, every harsh word adds a new brick to the wall of self-defense. After his constant string of criticisms about her hair, the way she spoke, the slight softness of her thighs, she built up a wall that now must be as long and as thick as the Great Wall of China.

"You look like your dog just died," Cara says scooting the *kir royale* toward her on the shiny metal table. Its pink bubbles rise up to the surface releasing giddy little whiffs of black currant and sparkling wine.

"That play," Vicki said reaching for the glass. "It makes me feel like I'm missing something. That there's something there that I didn't get."

"Maybe you'll have an 'ah-ha' moment when you least expect it. That happened to a stockbroker friend of mine. He woke up one morning and suddenly everything looked different. Said he couldn't explain it to anyone but he totally loved everyone and everything for no reason. But forget it. Let's have some fun." Cara smiles and winks at some young men. "I think they're watching us," she says. "I wonder if any of them owns a boat?" Vicki's mind agonizes over her acute sense of isolation.

"How's Old France?"

Vicki groans. She calls her boss "Old France" because he always wears Hermes ties, Dior suits, and owns an apartment near the Champs Elysees. Traditional, snobby, and condescending, he imagines himself above everyone. And he only seems to put stock in appearances, decorum, and power over others. "Same old, same old. I can never say or do the right thing around him. He'll never change."

"Well, he may not, but you can. You can always get a new job. Or change your attitude."

Her lips pucker. "I'm ready to go home," Vicki says. "It's been a long day."

"You can't," Cara pleads. "We just got here." She holds her glass up for a toast. "To love and friends," she says. A warm smile spreads across her tanned cheeks.

Vicki forces a smile. "Sure, whatever."

Cara's enthusiasm refuses to be dulled by Vicki's sullen mood. "I know what you need," she says suggestively. Vicki rolls her eyes.

"You mean sex?"

"How long's it been? Three months? Is that when you and Theo broke up?" Cara says.

Vicki clears her throat. "What good would it do?" she says.

"It'll be like a facelift. Have you looked at yourself in the mirror recently? Your lips are pinched. It would make you relax and smile a little. I read it takes up to seven years off your looks."

Vicki crosses her arms over her chest and rolls her eyes again. "I don't have pinched lips."

"Or buy a vibrator. They don't break your heart," Cara says.

Vicki laughs. "I think I'm going to go to the mountains tomorrow."

"Why's that?'

"To get a new perspective. From up there, you can see things differently. You can see for miles and miles. Maybe something will click. Want to come? I'll leave early."

"On a Sunday morning? No way. I'll be sleeping in as late as possible. If I'm lucky my sister will bring me chocolate croissants and make me a cappuccino. I won't have to get out of bed until noon!"

***

On Sunday, the sun greets Vicki like the bright, cheery face of a blonde two-year-old kid. The Sirocco wind that howled during the night polished the sky clear and bright. The terrace below her bare feet is splotched with orange-red sand that blew all the way across the Mediterranean from the Sahara. She yawns, stretches, and feels the mountains at her back. Her reflection stares back at her in the window. "Pinched lips, huh?" She touches a finger to her mouth. "Okay," she mumbles, looking down at the empty streets. "Let's go get a new perspective." A seagull swoops past and screeches out support. "Go," it says. She picks up her cell phone and types out a text message to Cara. "Okay lazy bones. Going to the Gorges while you sleep. Promise to seek new perspective. Sorry about being such a bore last night. XO. V." She doesn't bother to text anyone else. Who would be up at this hour on a Sunday anyway? Instead, she fills her backpack to the brim with a plaid blanket, chilled water, salad in Tupperware, and some chocolate cookies. She throws her hiking boots over her shoulder and heads down the stairs.

The car waits by the curb and she tosses her boots and pack onto the floor, jumps in, and shifts into gear. A woman with long dark hair ambles across the pedestrian crossing and flashes a smile at her. She looks oddly like the woman from the psychic fair, the one who predicted that a new experience would change her. Vicki's eyes squint, and she raises a hand to shelter them from the bright light. The familiar looking stranger waves and Vicki waves back. The words return, "You feel like no one has ever understood you." But what if the important thing is for her to understand others, or at least to try? Cara would be proud about her new point of view, and yet a sense of anticipation mixed with dread accompanies the thought. Maybe separation is good. Maybe it's easier to be isolated and alienated, to keep up the walls.

Driving the highway toward Grasse, Vicki's thoughts turn inward. No spoken words today, no conversations. Words are sometimes the problem, she thinks. Words that people say but don't mean. Words that mean one thing to her and another to someone else. She thinks of Theo who used to say, "I love you," when what he really meant was, "I want you, or I lust after you." And of her response, "Me too," which disguised her deep affection and love for him. She had desired to possess and love him so intensely that it would annihilate all traces of his past lovers. She turns off the highway onto the narrow village road leading up to the Gorges du Verdon, a canyon like a gaping mouth, where a river meanders through a deep valley cut out by the devastating twins of time and erosion. The air feels softer, gentler as she ascends into the mountains. The French Grand Canyon, some call it. It is surrounded by lush trees and the lavender scents of Provence.

At the dam people in canoes paddle around on glistening

water the color of fluorite. She passes a few bikers who wear tight black shorts and racing helmets. They lean into the curves of the winding road and zip along with ease. When the first stone cliffs appear, Vicki relaxes, breathes in the mountain air still cool from the morning dew. She winds her way along the rim of the canyon looking for the path. Ribbons of thin dark road wind up under her tires for miles. Trees and stony cliffs edge slowly past her until the little town of Moustiers appears. A star hangs on a chain suspended between two cliffs next to the church like a good omen from a medieval fairytale. Shop owners bend back their wooden plank doors and carefully lay out hand-decorated vases, bowls, and plates on tables and stands. Genies and animals smile out of the plates like sprites and fairies with human heads, animal torsos, and legs of vine and plant. A little river slides down the mountainside and cuts the town in two, but a kindly old bridge made of ancient stones allows her to cross over the gap.

On the other side, a herd of sheep block the way. The herder, with a long-haired dog that resembles a white bear, nudges the sheep onto the shoulder to let her pass. She smiles and waves thanks. The herder raises his hand grudgingly; his worn and weathered face remains stern, like a baked clay pot that might crack should he attempt to smile. A few kilometers on, she finds the path and edges the car into a narrow parking space on the shoulder of the road. She turns off the engine. A bird twitters a light, airy song, and the car fan whines to cool the motor. A plane yawns sleepily in the distance and leaves a white trail of jet stream.

She grabs the backpack and walks down the trail that descends about one-hundred feet over hard white stone. The path curves down to follow along the whitewater rapids. It passes through a short tunnel in the rock cliff where her eyes adjust, and the black shadows totally consume her before the light streams in at the opposite end. At the entrance to the second tunnel she reaches into her pack, finds the flashlight stored there, and flicks it on. Bats and vipers hang out in the tunnels, so she sweeps the beam back and forth to be on the lookout. Drops of moisture fall from the stone ceiling and trickle down her tank top. She shivers and the hair on her arms stands at attention. Her fingers skim the cool, damp stone walls as she feels her way through the darkness. We go in and out of periods of darkness and light, she thinks, like a series of tunnels. Black and white; darkness leads to light. But most of the time we linger in the shadows and gray areas in between, she thinks. When the light reappears and illuminates the slick stone arch of the tunnel she feels unusually happy. Sun rays fall on her bare shoulders and neck smoothing away the goose bumps, making her skin tingle with warmth. Along the river, she crosses a narrow footbridge. The steep canyon walls above her pin her in and she stands at a cross road. One path goes up, rocky and steep, but promises a way out, above the wall. The easier path ambles along the river. It's even, well-worn, and requires little effort, but it remains confined to the shadows of the granite cliffs where rays of light rarely touch the bottom.

"Okay," she says aloud. She decides to change perspective and climb up and out. The path narrows. She holds fast to the branches of small trees to help her anchor firmly and pull herself up to the next hold to reach higher ground. Stones fall away under her feet. She picks her way carefully up the path until she meets with a steel cable that runs about twenty-five feet straight up the wall, separating her from the peak. To reach the top, she will have to walk up the cliff vertically, her face turned to the sky, her arms and shoulders supporting her weight.

Turn back or go on? She wonders. She stops, sips from the water bottle, and looks at the white river several hundred feet below. The river looks like a narrow dark serpent from here. Up above, the sky glows deep blue, and a white cloud reflects light so intensely that she shields her eyes from its brightness. It's harder to go up, but she can't bear the thought of going back to the high walls.

Okay, she decides. I'll climb out. Her hands grip the steel cable firmly, and she anchors her right foot against the stone wall. She reaches up a foot higher with her left hand and her left foot meets the wall. If she did not know the distance below, it would be easy and even fun, but her legs begin to tremble from fear and her arms feel weak. She takes a deep breath and moves forward anyway, not recognizing a difference between courage and sheer will power. She just knows that she has to go on; she has to prove she can do it; she has to climb out of this hole and get above the cliffs.

More rocks fall away under her feet, but she braces herself. For a moment she looks down at the white boulders and water below. A rush of adrenaline sends her heart into high gear. Her body speeds up, and in an instant, she heaves herself up and collapses onto a grassy knoll. She lies on her back feeling spent but exhilarated. As she stares at the sky, clouds float by, shifting and changing forms: a fish, a dragon, a camel, and faces. She slips into an altered state, not quite asleep, yet not fully awake. Staring into the blue sky, tiny globules of light dance and dart about in the air like squiggles appearing and disappearing.

Vicki feels breathless, happy for no reason. Her breath deepens and a feeling of joy begins to permeate her fingertips and toes. Her cells tingle, vibrant and alive, like after a plunge in a cold mountain stream. A small bird flies overhead and a companion joins it. She perceives pale blue circles of light around them and wonders at the mystery of this revelation. They must be auras, she thinks. As the birds fly closer, the blue circles of light around them merge to form one bigger circle that encompasses both. When a third bird joins them, the circle enlarges to include them all. Vicki's eyes widen with awe. "Not separate, but one," she thinks, and the dullness she's felt for months disappears.

The world seems guided by some deep invisible pattern, some purpose and sense that is just out of view, just out of grasp, and yet… The clouds gather into white puffy balls of luminous silk. A thin wisp of clouds create a rainbow of thin voile around the sun, making Vicki wonder at the beauty and strangeness of perceiving a rainbow without rain. An auspicious sign, she thinks, and she can almost begin to feel how Rumi could dance with so much joy at the nature of life.

A bird perched on a branch in a bush beside her sings in harmony with the bliss in her heart. Its sweet throaty song fills her. She loves the bird who gives its song without anticipating anything in return. So often people give, but usually at a high price. "I'll love you if you grow up to be a success." Or, "I'll love you as long as you're pretty." The bird's sweet, lilting song carries her thoughts away until her heart opens like a flower. Though her eyes are closed, she feels the bird's heartbeat. Its heart beats fast, small, so alive! She feels it. She *is* it. Her eyes close in love and wonder. One heart, not two, in a moment transcendent of thought, of time, of being. She becomes the bird and the bird is in her, no longer separate but one and the same. The barriers fall. Like a drop of water losing its surface tension. They merge in the vast ocean of conscious awareness. The energy of love flows between them as natural and as freely as breath. Then her eyes jerk open. She scrambles up. Startled. Holds her breath. Oh my god, she thinks. This is not possible! Reason rushes in to rebuild the fences between her and the bird, to put mortar between the cracked wall of bricks built by ego and reason. How is it possible to feel another heart? She wonders. The bird darts away, as it too seemed to realize the merging, and then the sudden, spasmodic moment of separation. The spell is broken, but the experience cannot be denied.

Vicki's mind does not understand, yet her heart understands. For an instant their hearts had beat as one. She felt the bird, knew its heart, its joy in song, its fear when it flew off. But her mind refuses, denies, protests. We are condemned to live forever separate and alone, that's the way it has always been, she thinks. But her

inner wise-woman knows differently and cannot ignore the experience. By some strange occurrence, a conjunction of time and place,
or a blip in space, a fusion occurred. They merged, more intimate
than lovers, closer than twins in the womb, more connected than
the umbilical-corded baby and its mother. A perplexed joyfulness
invades her, and a brick in the wall of her subtle, but thick fortress
of self-protection falls to the ground. A crack appears and the wall
begins to crumble. "It's okay if no one understands me," she decides. "I will make the effort to understand them, to walk in their
shoes a few miles, to imagine how they feel. And I'll try to give
love for no reason, like the sun shines on me just because that's its
nature."

She packs up her blanket and hums as she walks back down the
path, back through the tunnels, back into the world of separation.
When she emerges into the light again, she feels oddly at peace.
Is there some invisible connection between people and birds and
things that is so mystical and profound that it remains hidden from
common knowledge? Connection this profound, she reasons, could
create a revolution. She climbs back into the comfortable cocoon of
her car and drives home, leaving behind the bird, the whispering
river, and the clouds filled with faces. As the streets grow larger
and more populated, reason once again drives her onward into a
one-dimensional world, wedged away from the interconnections,
away from her Self, back to her varying degrees of separation.

***

On Monday, she gathers with a group of secretaries at their usual
table at the *Antipolis Café* decorated with teak chairs and yellow
cushions. Leftover pizzas with mozzarella gelling to a hard
consistency sit half eaten on thick white plates.

"Do you know why it takes one million sperm to fertilize
an egg?" Sam, the blond part-time secretary, part-time massage

therapist says.

"Oh no, Sam's got another one," Cara says. The girls titter in anticipation.

"Is this another one of your dumb men jokes?" Vicki says.

Sam smiles infectiously, about to spill out laughter. "Because they refuse to stop and ask for directions." The girls laugh.

Vicki moans. "It's so true. Old France was in his usual form this morning," she announces. "He never actually asks for anything. I'm expected to be a mind reader instead."

"Maybe he should hire one of those clairvoyants like we saw this weekend," Cara says.

"You guys saw clairvoyants?" Sam says.

"She did." Vicki jerks her thumb in Cara's direction.

"I'm told I'm going to meet a man with a boat soon," Cara boasts.

"I could introduce you to my nephew Jason. He's got a toy boat that he loves to play with in the bath." Jeanette says. Cara rolls her eyes. "You should've seen M&M this morning."

"You mean Macho Marcus," Cara adds. "That's why you're in a bad mood."

"The one and only. He was strutting around barking out orders," Jeannette continues.

"Must not have gotten laid this weekend," Sam says.

"Really," Vicki says. "Maybe Old France has the same issue. Any volunteers to help him out?"

The group groans in collective disapproval. "Today he was his usual loveable self," she adds. "He came in and ripped up the report I prepared for him and threw it on the floor. If one of you guys would sacrifice yourself for the cause, it might make my life easier." She looks at her watch. "Gotta go." Vicki waves apologetically. Cara leaps up and grabs her by the arm.

"I'm going too." When they're a few feet away from the group, Cara whispers, "Old France may be in his usual rotten mood, but you look radiant. What happened?"

"Oh, nothing really." How can you explain that you've felt a bird's heart and merged with the canyon, the river, the sky? How do you talk about the walls that fell and how you became one with a bird?

"You didn't meet someone? You know…have sex?"

"No, of course not. I was alone."

"Oh," Cara says with meaningful understanding. "I do that sometimes too. You know when I really need it."

Vicki punches her arm. "It wasn't like that. It's just…something," she hesitates. "…a little unusual. I can't explain it. It was kind of Rumi-esque." Cara's eyes grow large in amazement.

"Whatever it was, you should do it more often."

"I went to the mountains. That's all. It was good to get away."

"See you later," Cara calls out.

"To love and friends," Vicki says. She holds up an imaginary glass in an airy toast.

Cara looks back and raises her imaginary glass in return.

***

Back in the serene box of the marble-floored office hemmed in with mahogany trim, Vicki sips a cup of coffee and concentrates on the travel plans to arrange for Old France. Curt, tight-lipped, officious, he knows about boundaries and builds up a fence with "Keep Out" signs hung all around. He rarely smiles except for a forced, insincere teeth-showing with clients, and he stinks of Monte Cristo cigar smoke. Once she tried to think of his good qualities, of a kind word to defend him when one of the other secretaries criticized, but no matter how hard she searched, nothing came to mind. He yelled and insulted employees, told dirty jokes, and never took her out for secretary's day. She only stayed with him because he paid her too much to leave.

He buzzes her through a wired system that lights up beside her desk, like someone might buzz for a bell boy or a maid. She grabs a notepad and shuffles to his door. Outside a box with buttons waits at eye-level by the door. She pushes a button to let him know she's waiting, and a series of three lights offer a response. "Please wait," "Do not disturb," and "Come in." Of course he would never actually get up to actually greet her at the door. "Come in," lights up and buzzes. As soon as the door opens he booms, "Where are my travel arrangements?" Three neat stacks of files line up on his antique oak desk.

"You mean for the 19th?"

"No, for tomorrow." He looks preoccupied. His face is taut with anger. "I'm sure I told you. 'Book 9:05 flight to Paris.'"

She knows he didn't tell her about it. "I'm sorry, sir."

"Meeting at Omni-Gen." He heaves back in his chair with a condescending snort. "Have to do everything myself."

"I'll take care of it."

"Do that." He puffs on his fat cigar, which forms a thick, grimy cloud in the air around them. "Get on it right now. And take this." Cigar smoke punctuates each word. He pushes a thick black binder of freshly signed documents at her.

She picks up the black binder and coughs as the gray cloud surrounds her. "Anything else?" she asks. He waves her away, and she closes the door, edging the handle down gently so that it will make no noise. Walls, doors, barriers – these are the easy, palpable things. They can be blown off hinges, opened and closed. Fences can be cut through; walls can be knocked down. But the invisible barriers around hearts? She thinks of the flying birds and their bluish circles of light. She tenderly remembers the birds too. She loved the song bird. It was love that made the difference, that made their hearts merge. She walks back to her desk, soaked in the unpleasant scent of his cigar and bad humor. She picks up the phone to retrieve the flight information, then returns to his door and the buzzer. She buzzes and waits for the signal. The sign lights up. "Please wait." And then it shifts to "Come in." She pushes back the door.

"There's a waiting list only for the 9:05 flight to Paris, Orly. I've put you on that. The other option is a 6:30 a.m. flight to Charles de Gaulle."

"If you would've gotten on it earlier..." He flips her away again. "That's all."

"I'll confirm for 6:30?"

"Yes," he grumbles, blows more thick smoke into the air and concentrates on dropping an inch of ash into the crystal ashtray, ignoring her. "Pray that the 9:05 opens up," he threatens through gritted teeth.

Late in the afternoon a call comes, a woman's voice, gentle, but serious. She wants to speak to Old France, strictly personal. Her name is Doctor Dennis, she says. In a few minutes he buzzes again. Vicki walks to the door and they go through their familiar routine.

"Cancel the flight for tomorrow." His tone is sullen; the air looks dim and leaden. A pang of fear invades her as if from outside, but she has no reason to feel afraid. Is she feeling his fear?

"And your meetings?"

"Cancel them too." Withdrawn, darker than before, he turns toward the window. The lights are out now except for a brass desk lamp that throws dark shadows on his face. His skin looks ashen. The ashtray is full of dust. He ponders a fat, unlit cigar between his finger and thumb. A hint of concern crinkles his eyes. She waits, notepad perched in hand. A shift, some tiny increment of change, a layer of the onion skin of separation that divides them peels away. Something changes in his eyes and she feels a heaviness. And his heart, is it trembling? She edges closer to see, to study the new twitch at the corner of his eye.

"Can I do anything, sir?" she asks gently.

The gentleness in her voice pierces the brittle air and dissolves the frigid distance. He focuses on her eyes a brief instant and she sees a vulnerable human being staring back at her. He appears confused and afraid, as if he's hoping to make sense of something it seems. Then in the intense intimacy of the moment, his cheeks flush. His eyes veer to the blinds and search out the light.

"That will be all." He chokes the words out.

She tip-toes out the door and closes it quietly. Something, a hurt, a dread, an illness, something has jumped upon him like a merciless bear about to tear his world to shreds. And oddly, she feels it; she knows. She wants to knock on his door again and tell him not to worry. But instead she does her duty, cancels the meetings, and decides to go home to finish the day. She buzzes, speaks into the speaker. "Is there anything else before I go?"

"Yes. Come here," followed by a word he rarely uses. "Please."

She walks to his door again. "You may not be able to reach me tomorrow." He stops, hesitates. "Tests and such." His voice jerks and drags over the words as if they are a death sentence.

"Oh, I am sorry." And she truly is. It resounds in her voice.

"It's nothing."

She understands the fear and vulnerability she'd sensed from him earlier, and now she feels his dread, his fear perhaps of positive tests and exploratory surgery. Her heart trembles too and she remembers the bird and the mystical heart to heart connection. A sudden, inexplicable feeling of compassion flows out from her chest. His hand lays limp on the desk. She reaches out and touches it. For an instant she dares to be strong and powerful enough to let the barriers fall and let love flow without conditions. He looks up surprised and embarrassed. For a moment he looks stunned and

tears form in his eyes like he will cry. He squeezes her hand in return and she detects an urge in him to hold on to her like a lifeline.
But he clears his throat, pulls his hand away, and returns to focus
on some papers.

"You can go now."

"Yes, sir," she says.

He looks up and away quickly as she glances over her shoulder
on her way out, and then closes the door. She takes a few steps. A
buzz comes from behind her. "Come in," the light blinks. She eases
open the door and smiles at him as if he's playing a joke. His wall
breaks a little too. The corners of his lips turn up just a hint, so that
anyone who didn't know him as well as she did might mistake
it for a grimace caused by gas. A stream of light pierces through
the blinds lighting the space between them, and the intimacy of
unspoken understanding engulfs them. Just as quickly as he took
off the hard-faced mask, he puts it on again. He heaves his chair
back under the desk and speaks in a dry, neutral tone. "It's strictly
confidential."

"Yes, I understand." Her voice still sounds soft and soothing.

"Good evening," he says, and they are back to normal, back to
the usual cool, safe distance.

But outside his door, Vicki smiles at herself and shakes her
head. Another brick in the imaginary wall that separates her from
others falls at her feet and she leaves it on the ground. She marvels
at how she had felt his dread and knew that something was wrong,
how she reached out and it was okay. Her heart opens wider. A soft
bright light pierces through the office blinds and illuminates her
path like a ray of sun at the end of a long, dark tunnel.

Chapter 6
Six O'clock at Eden Roc

At six o'clock, I have the place to myself – except for the chef, Maxime, who drinks sherry and paces back and forth. What am I doing here, you wonder. Sixteen, Moroccan, but light skinned thanks to my French mother from Metz. I polish etched crystal glasses – Baccarat, they say – and line up the real silver silverware two centimeters out from the plates like Luigi showed me. Dinner fork, salad fork, knives. You'd think it was a science or something, when in a couple of hours they'll all be dirtied, including the white linen tablecloths and napkins.

I get nervous when they're all here – the big shots with their kids and dogs. But mostly it's old people – retired people or silver-haired guys with girlfriends who look like models. I study them, look into their eyes – those girls – and they look away. I know I shouldn't do it. The boss says we don't make eye contact. It's an affront. It puts us on the same level as them – a level where we don't belong – especially me. So it's like a game. We're supposed to blend into the background so they can have a smooth experience. But he catches me watching sometimes, and the boss slaps me on the back of the head when we get in the kitchen. But so far, most of the time, I keep out of trouble.

"Jamal!" That's the chef yelling. "We're out of sherry." That means go down to the cellar and get him more. The keys to the stores hang in the kitchen cabinet and I grab them. "No fooling around down there," Maxime snaps.

I salute him. "Yeah, chef."

I seen them guys, the kitchen staff, hanging around the stores usually trying to pocket what they can. One guy carries off silverware. Every few days he slips a fork or spoon into his vest pocket and sneaks away with it. "The wife wants a full set," he chuckled when he caught me watching. I guess I must've had my mouth gaping open, because he whined, "Everybody does it." I kept on arranging the clean glasses on the tables, not looking into his face. "Don't think you're better than I am, boy. It'll infect you too. You can't help but become sick or a thief from all the money floating around here. It's unhealthy, fills you with too many desires and too much envy." And disgust, I wanted to say – like when that family of dress-wearing sheiks came in and let their naked baby son run around and crap on the carpet. Luigi sent me to clean it up of course – and all those Arab brothers laughed and pointed at me. I'm one of you, I wanted to say, then I realized I'm not really. I've got less money, but more manners.

I'd only been there at the Hôtel a few weeks then. But I sensed what that guy meant. My mouth watered at the thick, juicy steaks smothered in hollandaise sauce with mushrooms, and the chocolate mousse cakes topped with gold leaf. None of it like anything I'd ever seen before and none of it for us, of course. But at least I have the luxury of being here, of seeing another life. An old lady wrapped in diamonds and mink came in alone with her dog a few nights ago. A dog. Here. Sitting on the chair at her table at the Eden Roc restaurant! And she ordered two filets. Luigi, the head waiter, turned red when he had to cut up one steak in bite-sized pieces for her Pekinese. A one-hundred fifty euro steak for that dog! "Surprised she didn't serve him wine too!" Luigi muttered bitterly afterward. Luigi's been around a long time and seen a lot of stuff. My mouth watered from the smell sizzling off that beautiful piece of meat – and the dog with a bow and silver collar licked his chops and ate it from the old lady's Christofle fork right at the table. They have a pet cemetery too, out in the garden. One with a sea view. The lucky dog will probably end up buried there.

But the view's a knock-out. God, can you believe it? I mean how many kids my age get to set foot at the Hôtel du Cap? Just going to the pool costs eighty-five euros. It's sea water, of course. A coffee costs five times more here than at the café down the street. But they don't mind it. The millionaires want to hang out behind the gates. They want privacy, and when you've got millions a few euros don't really count. I saw Madonna when she booked in. She took the boat from the pier. She didn't want to be caught up in crowds waiting for a glimpse outside the gates. She had a *sosie*, *a* look-alike who stayed here and acted as a sort of decoy to fool people so the real Madonna could get away to do what she wanted.

Tonight, an icon film star is coming. We're not supposed to know, but Maxime couldn't help but complain about the special requests. The guy's girlfriend's a vegan, whatever that is. Sounds like some extraterrestrial life form. "Only raw stuff, no meat, eggs, fish or cheese," Max gagged. "Ah *mon dieu*! What am I? A chef for rabbits? The woman needs a good screw. It would give her an appetite for real food," he said. Luigi liked this, looked even like he might volunteer for the job. And there's also the reception on the terrace. Another group of guys – a once famous boy band are releasing a new album. A new start – and they're doing a little pre-launch party here with the producer, like a celebration, Luigi says.

"If I could live like them…" Luigi sighs. His voice trails off. He saw all the Arabs come with the oil boom, and then the Russian mafia, and of course the Americans – always the Americans and now the Chinese. But Luigi says it's not the place for new money. It's mostly old money – people with names, and histories, and families. He says the Kennedys came too. "I am going to live like them someday," I tell him and he rolls his eyes.

The sun sets over in that direction, over the islands out there. Every once in awhile I find myself staring out, fantasizing, thinking about what I'll be when I get older. I'm not going to stay here doing this stuff forever, you know. I've got ambition. First a *commis* during the seasons here, then in the winters move to the five stars in the mountains, maybe Courchevel. Once you get a reputation for big places, you've got to keep it up. Mom says I should go back to school in the winters, but making this much money – a heck of a lot more than she gets from the *RMI* –how can I quit? I'm just lucky that Max liked me, that he said okay. Luigi says the only reason I got hired as Max's assistant (he never takes Maghrébins, Luigi says, they don't like North Africans) is because Max likes the looks of me, wants my ass. Luigi says I'm a looker to those kinds of guys, but I think he's got a weird imagination. Yeah, Max had a funny look in his eye alright; a shiny, strange look when he hired me, but too much sherry does that to a guy, I guess.

Luigi says, "Get some experience with the world, kid. But don't expect too much. That's my philosophy," he says. "That way I never get let down." Luigi pocketed a tin of caviar after a big banquet too. "Go ahead and take some," he insisted. "Who's going to care?"

I knew my mom would. I did spread some on a biscuit though and took a bite. Gross stuff, so salty and the little eggs popping in your mouth. Luigi laughed. I liked the petit fours though and ate my share of them once the whole thing was over. Max said I could. He even gave me a few to take home for mom.

I was feeling pretty good about the world up until a couple

of days ago when that blonde girl came. She must be young, but mature for her age, like me. Her huge, watery eyes beg for help or something. I felt a pang in my stomach the first time she flashed that look. A queer excitement raced up to my heart. And now I can't get her out of my mind. The guy who looks like an old fella, her dad, or an uncle maybe, makes her walk out of the restaurant ahead of him with his hand at the small part of her back, but she keeps staring back, looking at me staring at her. At lunch, they sat out by the pool today. She wore a white bikini and looked like a goddess. The old man couldn't keep his eyes away – like maybe he was afraid she might escape or something. And when she saw me watching this afternoon, she slyly flashed the edge of a smile and showed perfect, white teeth like pearls, and then she looked straight at me. She smiled at *me*. But I caught myself. Not allowed to smile back. What if Luigi or Max saw, or her old man? That would be the end of me.

***

The sun's about to dip into the water now. It's almost like you can hear or imagine the sizzle as its fire goes out in the sea. Sssssszzzz. That pinkish-red ball hangs there and then dives. I imagine someone flicks a huge, gold Cartier lighter in the morning to bring it back to life. The lights go up inside the restaurant and the faces of clients lit with candles makes them look ghoulish and old with shadows. The film icon comes in as if on cue – unshaven, wearing holey jeans, a dirty t-shirt, like a zombie coming out of a cemetery still covered with grime. And Luigi has to serve this slob all the same, just because he's got money, and a name. He looks like a bum. Any other guy they'd kick out. They'd call the police, but this guy flaunts it. He makes Luigi kiss his ass and his girlfriend's. This is what makes Luigi sick. "I'm going to retire soon, before I end up smashing someone in the teeth," Luigi whispers to me between gritted teeth.

The girl comes back, the blonde with her dad. A loose, lilac chiffon top billows over her jeans. She's a knock out. My chest feels tight like a steel band's around it, and I hardly breathe. "Don't just stand there. Go serve them water," Luigi hisses. "Sparkling." I jump out of the spell and go – hurry to the bar, without looking hurried. It's to keep the atmosphere smooth – no jerks or rough starts. No screw-ups allowed. The bartender rips off the metal cap with a hiss and hands the bottle to me. I walk to their table, watching the girl, then I try not to watch her. But as the water splashes into their glasses – the biggest one's for the water – she picks up her linen napkin and brushes the edge of my hand – accidentally. Or maybe not, and our eyes meet and she smiles, a big childish smile full of what? Expectation? I quickly put the bottle into the ice bucket and slip away. My hands shake; my heart thumps. Oh my god, such beauty. I've never met anyone so beautiful. She must be a starlet or something.

The film star's bruise-eyed, vegan girlfriend throws a tantrum at the sight of Max's vegetable dish, *en croûte*. It looks like a piece of art – with julienne of thinly sliced carrots on the side, green micro herbs, and field flowers. "Nothing cooked!" she huffs and throws her fork on the floor to protest. "Oh go to hell," her boyfriend mutters and cracks the claws of a thick-shelled lobster. "Just ignore her," he says as a way of apologizing to Luigi. Luigi wavers back and forth not knowing who to side with, then backs away. "Just bring her a head of lettuce that she can munch on." Luigi doesn't know if this is a serious order or not. Sometimes people ask for strange things here. The icon helps him out. "Just bring her a salad."

"The icon has spoken," Luigi says to Max returning to the kitchen. "His pronouncement is that the woman must be laid, but he's too drugged to do it. Wants to know if you're man enough."

"Oh spare me the disgusting details," Max barks.

"*Pédé,*" Luigi hisses.

"What are you sneering at?" Max barks at me. "You little girl." He shakes his butcher's knife and I scurry out. The party outside with the producer and his boys flickers out early. Everybody stands around with half-empty glasses looking bored before slipping away and leaving the main man alone with a chatty red-head. "Life sucks," Luigi says, imitating the producer's English accent. "Those guys are bad news."

"Yeah, bad news boys, ha ha," I say making a play on their name. I carry a silver tray of finger sandwiches to the buffet. An ice carving of the boys stands over the table melting away like their fame. When I go back, the blond girl's on her way out again and she looks beat, with dark circles and red eyes. Maybe she was crying. When she sees me staring, I feel she's begging for help, like she wants to be rescued from that guy (who maybe isn't her father after all) – maybe even from herself, and I don't know what to do. So I ignore it and walk into the kitchen where Luigi rolls out the trolley of desserts.

***

When the night's over, I'm dead. My feet hurt. My legs hurt. Luigi says it gets worse when you get older. But I won't be doing this much longer. Max has already gone – retired to his room upstairs. He's one of the lucky ones who gets a room here – at least until the end of the season when the whole place closes down, boarded up and deserted like a ghost town. Sheets on the yellow satin furniture, and all the beds will be stripped naked. I step out back for a minute. "Smoking's not good for you," Luigi grumbles, then lights up one too.

"Yeah? Look at you."

"I'm old enough that it doesn't matter."

"Besides, I only smoke one or two."

"Me too."

"Liar."

Luigi stubs out his cigarette. "Back to work, kid."

The ember dies under the heel of my black leather shoe, the ones that the hotel makes me wear. Part of the uniform, they say. Part of the class they sell. The boys from the band have mostly dribbled away with model-girlfriends on their arms, and the bar is about to close. The restaurant is empty except for the icon who scrapes his girlfriend out of her seat and pulls her toward the door. She collapses in a heap on the thick carpet and he leaves her there. "Ah, fuck it," he says and walks away.

The woman lies there blubbering about miserable life. "Go pick her up. Take her to her room," Luigi says.

I point back at my chest with my index finger and mouth "me?", and look at her like she's toxic. "I'm not going to do it. She's vegan," I say like it's some disease.

He glares at me and I finally walk to the lady sprawled by the door, her hair strung over her face, and slip her arm over my shoulder. "Fucking bastard. He's a fucking bastard. He makes me sick," she says. Her words slur together, but she manages to stand up on her skinny legs and wobble along beside me.

"What's your room number, ma'am?"

"You wanna fuck me? He won't do it. You wanna?" She puts her slimy lips on my cheek.

"Luigi, what's the room number?"

"Twenty-one." He looks at me sly-like, like he's got something over on me. Everybody hates a drunken woman slobbering on herself. So he pushed the job off on me. Up at the room, the door's open a crack. It's a suite – all couches and silk pillows and thick shiny drapes. The icon's naked. "Deposit her in there." He points to an adjoining room, where I spot clothes, shoes, dirty underwear, and used syringes on the bedside table. Looks like a war zone. So this is the lap of luxury. Limp as a noodle, the woman flops on the bed. I don't cover her or anything with the guy there watching me.

"Here kid." He hands me fifty-euros and shoves me out the door. "You didn't see anything," he says. "You talk to any reporters and I'll personally fuck you up." He makes a strangling motion with his hands.

"No sir. Thank you, sir." In the hall my chest feels all tight from the nerves. My knuckles itch too. Then the girl pops out, the blond goddess with torn lilac chiffon. Tears stream down her cheeks and she clutches at herself. I can't help myself. "You okay?" I say. She looks pitiful. Her eyes turned up with that begging look. Bruises stain her bare arms. "Did he do that?"

"Leave me alone," she says and stands there, arms crossed over her chest waiting for something, maybe for him to come out and find her.

"Maybe I can help." I realize I'm staring down at her breasts visible under the transparent blouse, then straight into her eyes. An affront. It's forbidden. *We're not on the same level*, Luigi's words yell back at me.

"Who are you?" She sounds haughty, like she's on a pedestal looking down at me. "You're nothing more than a slave to me, a peon." Her hatred seethes out, tarnishing her beautiful face like a crack in a porcelain vase. And I'd thought she was beautiful. Her watch hangs open on her arm. A steely Cartier. I put my head down and walk away, leaving her barefoot and practically naked in front of his door.

Back in the kitchen, the stainless steel counters gleam and Luigi's got his pack of cigarettes in hand. "That girl, that blonde with the old man, he's not her father is he?"

Luigi's eating a *millefeuille* and spews out flakes of pastry in a cloud like he thinks I'm stupid or slow or something. "Her father?" And he starts to laugh really loud. I get the impression he's laughing at me. "You've got a lot to learn kid."

"She's his wife you think?"

"Sounds like you're love struck. Get her out of your mind. You don't have enough money to pay for a chick like that."

My cheeks heat up. "I don't think she's like that, Luigi." He can't stop laughing. "You just don't get it kid." He slaps me on the back. "Let's call it a night."

I slip out the door ahead of him and hop on my scooter. I liked her. I really did. I don't know why she acted that way. I wanted to help.

I feel really tired now, like I'm carrying a bag of lead on my shoulders. But tomorrow I get paid. Maybe tomorrow I'll buy a Cartier watch. The wind feels so cool on my face and that sea air makes me feel oh so alive. I gotta wonder about people like that. The icon, the drunk woman, the child-girl in the hallway, the kid crapping on the carpet.

Soon, I'll be there, in a place where they'll wait on me. And I don't want to create any misery. Someday soon I'll be a guest on the Cap and not just a *commis*.

Chapter 7

The Fires of St. Jean

"You can't go!" Gale says. A quiet desperation flashes through her eyes. Her hands tremble.

"You know I can't stay." Cara nudges her twin sister's elbow playfully. "Jump over the bonfire with me. It'll chase away your demons." The fire hisses and crackles in the center of the square. It's the festival of the summer solstice and the air feels balmy. Though it's evening, the sky's still filled with light dancing on the sea in front of them. *Saint Jean's* fire in the center of the plaza burns high and bright while the orchestra plays and the moon decorates the horizon like a giant opal.

Cara observes the people packed together, elbow to back to rump. Many of them hold plastic cups and seem tipsy from wine served at the street-side bars. Antibes' mayor announces the official start of summer and the *Fête de Saint Jean,* and the crowd roars and applauds. The first man bounds over the flames; his muscles ripple like those of a wild stag, and when he lands safely on the other side people applaud.

"Come on. Give it a try just once," Cara insists. "It may be our last chance. You never know where we'll be next year." Gale's green eyes widen with fright, and she shakes her head no. "O.K. Well, I'm going to get us some drinks," Cara says, aware of her own self-consciousness and a certain amount of dread at the idea of jumping. From the line behind the wooden hut on the other side of the fire, Cara observes Gale. Her arms hang limply at her sides and her head sinks into her shoulders. "Two glasses of rosé," she says to the vendor. Gale always drank white wine. But lately she's changed. Gale seems distant and moody. Cara observes her sister through the orange veil of fire that separates them. Streaks of light play on her face, casting deep shadows under her eyes making her look ghastly. Cara takes the drinks and works her way back around to the other side of the circle.

"When we were kids it seemed easier. Jumping, I mean. I thought we were immortal then," Cara says, returning to their conversation. It had been a family tradition.

"I always knew I'd fall." Gale shivers. "I wish dad hadn't made such a big deal." She stares down at her feet. "I wanted so much to please him. But I just couldn't." She exhales, her breath heavy with the metallic odor of stress.

"I felt I could conquer the whole world every time I jumped over it," Cara recollects. "For a little while at least."

"Things seemed so much simpler then," Gale sighs. Their eyes meet. Gale's eyes water. "I don't know what I'll do without you." Cara squeezes Gale's arm to reassure her and thinks of how she will miss her sister and this place too. She arches her back to view the two medieval stone towers that soar above them.

"I wonder if Picasso jumped over the fire when he lived up there?" Cara says.

"Too proud. Can you believe the city gave him that place to live in?"

"At least he left some art in exchange."

"Just a few drawings really. A pretty meager showing," Gale protests. "His best work like 'Night Fishermen' by the fortress should be here, not in New York." Cara fills her lungs with the crisp night air.

"Tourists come to visit it all the same. I wonder if Graham Greene ever stumbled upon our pagan fire rites when he lived down the street," Cara says. Talking of childhood love for literature, art and life is safe. It veers them away from the underlying anxiety about Cara's move to Spain.

"I don't know why people make a big deal about Greene or his books," Gale says.

"I like them. You know he lived next door to his lover and her husband," Cara says. Gale gazes into the flames and seems to travel off in her mind to a distant place, but Cara keeps up the chatter. "He also yearned to meet Padre Pio." Cara checks to see if Gale is listening.

"The Catholic priest with the stigmata?" Gale says turning her attention back to the present.

"Exactly. Greene waited for years. When he finally got an appointment to meet Pio face to face, he attended his mass just before. And you know he fled halfway through it, saying, 'I was not prepared for the way that man could have changed my life.' Can you imagine that?"

"Yes," Gale says.

"I think he feared change."

Gale sighs heavily and sips at her wine in a plastic cup. "It's hard to change."

"It's not." Cara says. "I'm proof. I'm changing jobs, cities…"

"Sisters," Gale says. Her pale, worn face closes up like a steel curtain shutting up a shop. Cara shakes her and wants to say, 'I'm sorry,' but checks herself. She doesn't feel sorrow, so she changes the subject. "Why don't you read anymore? It's better than all that TV junk. Or try to write or paint. You've always said you wanted to, and now that you have some free time..."

"Since Rod left, I can't sleep or anything," Gale says. Her voice sounds far away. "TV rests my mind, especially when I have insomnia." Gale yawns and her voice descends to a whisper. "Which is most of the time."

"Apparently you don't want anyone else to have the luxury of sleep either," Cara says gently, but she feels irritated as she recalls the TV voices booming through the walls of the house until after three a.m. last night.

"Oh," Gale says. "I wish you'd just yell at me instead of trying to be polite about it. It would make me feel better and you too. I know sometimes you could kill me."

"I love you, sis. I can't ever replace you." Cara wants to say more, but she bites her tongue and blocks the swell of emotions in her throat. "I hate to see you wasting your life. I mean you used to love to paint and dance and sculpt. You were so creative." Her voice cracks. Nothing Cara says seems to make a difference, but she tries anyway.

"Maybe I'll go and sit on the terrace at *Belles Rives* with my notebook like F. Scott Fitzgerald did. 'Another Scotch, *s'il vous plaît.*'" Gale's sarcasm replaces her dullness as she mimics his American accent. Her eyes drift out to the place where the walls meet the sea and encircle the old town. "Nicolas de Stael would understand," Gale says. Her face turns gray and she seems to withdraw to an inner sanctum filled with tempests and squalls. Cara remembers the carved stone memorial to de Stael at the edge of the window where he resided above the walls before he committed suicide.

"He was a cheater," Cara says. The melancholy grays and blues of de Stael's canvases capture the dark, waters that swell and slam against the old town's walls in December. She absorbs his somber mood and feels a momentary sadness and despair.

"At least he gave us his art," Gale says. The print of his *Fort Carée* hangs in Gale's living room.

A fortress to keep people out, Cara thinks. "There was nothing courageous about his choice," she says. An edgy hopelessness sidles in around them like a fog rising from a cold abyss, and the hairs on Cara's arms stand from the evening sea breeze. "Everybody else has to get on with life and live it, but he…"

"Opted out…," Gale says. "Life was too much. Maybe people hurt him and took him for granted…Maybe he was facing too many problems. Maybe he gave too much."

Cara's mind scurries about searching for a lighter subject, but she gives up and thinks of his madness. Why would anyone do that? She wonders. Did he become overwhelmed by suffering?

"I bet that solved a lot of things," Cara says. The sharp clarity of her voice cuts through the air. She faces the fire and the late evening sky still filled with bright, solstice light. It's the longest day of the year, their favorite day. But why doesn't it ever last? Cara thinks. She wants to cry out. Her heart aches with yearning for something permanent, an eternal sun that will not ever betray her. Her brow wrinkles until the bonfire flames leap high and the orchestra playing Pachelbel's *Canon* weave warmth around her like a soft blanket that drives away the chill. The fire fills Cara with delight like a warm companion on a summer night. Staring into its reddish-gold spears, she swears it has eyes that wink and shimmer and beckon her to draw near and try her luck.

"Sssss," it hisses. "Seeeiizeee," it says as if trying to pronounce a word.

No, it can't be, she thinks and returns to the vision of Gale's pale face in the shadows. "I wonder who started the *Fête*?" Cara says. Gale sips her wine, but is absent and seems to be a million miles away. Cara thinks of the faded sundials painted on the sides of old stone monuments still visible in the villages near Grasse. "Druids or pagans, I think. I'm sure they lived by the light. They must have been grateful to the fire. It's like a small piece of the sun."

Gale stirs. "I prefer darkness and winter nights."

"That's because you like to hibernate." Cara scans the crowd. Fire lights up the faces making even the elderly glow with a youthful, reddish tint. The postman who usually chatters incessantly halts beside others in reverent silence, paying tribute to the fire's mystical power.

"It's silly," Gale says. "And dangerous too."

Cara scans the faces again. "It's not silly. Just look around. It's our tradition."

"Maybe the Greeks found our forefathers here dressed in animal skins and bone necklaces, worshiping the light and jumping two thousand years ago." The people around her wear polo shirts and jeans or brightly colored shorts. Old men shift from foot to foot absorbing the power of the heat and watching; some couples jump together hand in hand and other people wait in line to build up courage. Those who dare to face it run and jump over the hot flames. Cara admires their courage and agility.

"It was our rite of initiation."

"Initiation into what? Terror?" Gale says.

"Into adulthood. It was living proof we had the courage to overcome obstacles, to show we could face fear and win. You'll have to bring Arielle and let her be part of this too."

"She's too young and her dad wouldn't agree. Besides, jumping over *that* doesn't prove anything!"

"How would you know? Every year you said you'd jump, but you never even tried." Gale bristles and steps away from her sister.

"One day I will. You'll see." Dark circles loom under her eyes like half moons and Gale's voice carries an undertow of threat. Cara ignores the menace. "You'll see," Gale adds. A certain determination and inner strength mark Gale's face, a subtle, but definitive shift into some new place of frightful courage or madness perhaps.

"Don't start," Cara warns and breathes a sigh to let off the tension built up between them. Gale often provokes and manipulates with her threats, but Cara hardens herself a little to keep her heart safe. Gale's eyes glimmer, reflecting the fire light, and the red eyes of some demon inside her seem to peer out. In a black t-shirt and slim white jeans someone might still mistake Gale for a hormone-troubled teenager, not a thirty-five year-old mother.

"I'll be gone in a few days," Cara says. "Let's just have fun and enjoy these precious moments together." The gentle breeze curls around them and rustles the leaves of the palms. Mozart's concertos lilt up and dance in the air. "The whole country's filling up with music tonight," Cara says. A few years ago, the French government declared the first day of summer as the *Fête de la Musique,* and together it merged with St. Jean's Day and its pagan origins. Around town and across France, orchestras, rock bands, and New Orleans jazz bands play on the streets, squares, and sidewalks. "I think it's a grand idea!" The notes from the violins of the black-suited orchestra on the *Place* lift her spirit. A hint of Pan's flute echoes out of a square behind them, and a harp soloist plucks at her angelic strings. Cara's heart wings skyward carried by the notes, up to the full, golden-pink moon. Emotions gather in her throat until she thinks she may burst. Love of this place, love for its history, for her sister and for life mingle with the frustration that it dissipates so quickly and unpredictably. Her eyes water from the poignancy and from bliss. Embarrassed, she turns her head away from Gale and swipes away the tears.

The wine weaves its magical spell of giddiness and a smile

wriggles across her lips. Cara feels finally, once and for all that she is happy – not for any reason or accomplishment or thing, but simply because she has decided to be now. Now and not later in some dreamy future when she will find the perfect mate, or land the ideal job, or own a bigger house. The drum beat of some boys playing bongos on the beach in the distance pound out the rhythm of her heart. The rhythm stirs up excitement and reminds her of the adventures awaiting her in Spain. Gale will have to make her own choice to be happy or not.

"It's so unbearably beautiful tonight. Just look around. Listen to the orchestra playing. Take it all in," Cara says. She opens her arms and her heart expands. Gale crosses her arms over her heart.

"I'm tired. I never liked St. Jean's Day anyway. Not then, not now," Gale announces flatly. But when they were kids she used to get as excited as most kids get for Christmas. She begged to come out for the *Fête*. Cara's mouth opens to protest, to remind her sister, but she decides not to argue and silently marvels at how their memory of a common past has diverged. Cara focuses on the good memories, Gale on the negative.

"You'll be out having fun, but I'll be all alone when you leave," Gale sighs.

"Try to be happy for me. I'll be doing something I love. Besides, you still have Arielle," Cara says. Gale's face darkens. She drains her glass and spills some wine on her chin.

"Rod wants to move to the U.S. with his girlfriend and my daughter." Gale's voice takes on a falsely light tone, but she nervously tears at the edge of her fingernail with her teeth.

"Oh how devastating! Why didn't you say anything before?" How long has this worry been smoldering inside her, Cara wonders. "Besides, he can't," she says. "You're her mother."

"He says I'm not taking care of her. He's trying to make a case that I'm no good. He's threatening to cut off child support."

Cara thinks of the ochre façade house with arcades and the small garden where they live. It used to be one big, open house with bay windows, but recently Gale has taken to keeping the shutters closed and locking the door between their adjoining apartments. "In case someone might break-in," Gale had said. "It would make it harder for thieves to penetrate both places." But Cara felt it meant something more. Cara lives on the ground floor, and often strolls out by the pool to save the occasional frog or bee that might fall in and otherwise drown. But Gale remains upstairs, locked inside, lying in bed until late in the day. Lately Cara hears Arielle's bare feet plod down the stairs on weekends, followed by a light knock on her wooden door. This morning, Arielle stood there with her bathrobe tied loosely, her seven-year-old face filled with confusion and fatigue.

"How about a good, strong coffee?" Cara said. Arielle wrinkled her nose.

"Uugghh."

"Scotch on the rocks?" Cara joked. Arielle rolled her eyes and groaned again. "I know, you prefer a stiff drink of chocolate milk!" Cara pulled her inside and tickled her until they collapsed in a giggling heap on the couch. "I bought some organic, frosted corn-flakes for you," Cara said. "Your favorite."

"Whatever." Arielle pretended to be unaffected by hunger or her mother's growing indifference. "I'm fine really," she said like a grown up. Cara cut up fresh mangos and strawberries all the same because she knew Arielle loved these most. She squeezed some fresh orange juice, and set it all on the mahogany table. Arielle ignored her and fiddled with the cat until it rolled over on its belly and purred. Finally she walked to the table and nibbled at the fruits, while the upstairs phone rang and people left messages: a friend calling to offer help; Arielle's father calling to speak to her; a salesman for windows.

Neither Arielle or Cara mentioned her sleeping mother. But
Cara could hear them at night through the walls. Arielle wept
while Gale harshly whispered threats and swore to go where
Arielle might never see her again. Any words about it from Cara
might draw out the child's fears, so she rubbed Arielle's shoulder
lightly as she passed instead. Cara imagined the inner workings of
Arielle's mind as she struggled to make sense of it: *How to make it
all better? Where's the magic wand to return things to normal? How can
I get my parents back together again? It must be my fault.*

"Staying with your dad tomorrow?" Cara said.

"Yes." The child spoke with precise words. "He's coming to get
me at ten. We're going to Monte Carlo for lunch tomorrow."

"Sounds like fun. Going shopping too?"

"We're going to the aquarium. The fish make me feel calm."
She reflected and picked at the fruit taking only the small, daintiest
bits. "Why are you leaving us?" Arielle said. Cara felt taken aback.

"Why, I have to. I can't lose this opportunity. You can come
to visit me. We'll learn Spanish together." The job in Barcelona
offered a promotion, a better salary and a new start. Maybe she
would meet a man, someone solid and even-tempered. Gale would
be jealous, of course. She wanted everyone for herself.

***

At the end of the evening when the fire burns with less rage, Gale
narrows her eyes. "St. Jean's ire is what it should be called."

"You're the only one who's angry," Cara says. She crosses her
arms over her chest.

"You would be too if everybody abandoned you!" Gale's face
twists up.

"If you're thinking of Dad, he didn't abandon you or me for
that matter. He died. Everybody dies. At his age it was normal,

better than average even." Their mother who had died when they were children lingers like a ghost too painfully close to the perimeter of their consciousness to be mentioned.

Gale rolls her eyes, loses a tear. "And Rod," she says. Her ex-husband left her for a tight-lipped American woman with a ranch in Texas. "How do you explain Rod?"

"Divorce happens to a lot of people. About fifty percent actually. Most people get on with their lives." But Gale cried every day for a year. "You will meet someone new, someone much better."

"So that's it. We're all replaceable." Gale broods.

Cara thinks of her ex-boyfriend's photo albums. She pictures the other women who had come and gone before, and how someday someone new might see a picture of her there too.

"Kind of seems that way," she says. "So you have to enjoy the moments as much as you can."

"But my therapist. How do you explain that?"

"Bad luck. I'm sure he would've preferred to keep going rather than keel over on the golf course from a heart attack."

"You don't understand." Gale glares.

"You're right. I think life's unfair and I don't understand why anyone has to die. But the world would be a pretty crowded place if we all lived forever."

"And now you. You're leaving too," Gale says flatly.

"I'm only going to Spain. It's a two hour flight away. Come and visit me." Her tone remains light, excited at the idea. "We could go to clubs together, maybe learn Salsa dancing. You might even meet a handsome Spanish man." She puts her hands in the air to imitate a Flamenco dancer.

"You don't understand," Gale repeats sullenly.

"Oh come on and lighten up," Cara says shaking her. But Gale pouts. "You're right," Cara says plunking her fists defiantly on her hips. "I don't understand why you stay in bed for days on end. And don't blame it on me."

"You don't love anyone," Gale says.

"You mean attachment, not love. No, I'm not attached to people. I don't hold on so tight that people suffocate." Gale turns away, dejected. Cara reaches out, touches Gale's shoulder, but Gale steps out of reach. "Let's just enjoy our last few days together."

"You think it's so easy," Gale says.

"Not really. I think it takes effort."

"Listen, I'm tired, I'm going back home. Maybe I can sleep now," Gale says distracted. "Mind if I take the car?"

"Please stay a little longer," Cara urges gently.

"I'm sorry." Gale says. Her face wrinkles with discomfort.

Cara feels guilty now. "I'm sorry if I said anything to upset you." Gale's mouth wrinkles as if she might cry. "It means a lot to me that you came tonight," Cara says. Her voice resounds soft and even.

"I need a hug, please." Gale says, tears in her eyes. Cara embraces her sister's frail body until she feels Gale resist and pull away.

"Be careful on your way home." Cara watches until she disappears. It feels like the cord that binds them stretches thin and snaps. A twinge of sadness and finality interrupt her festive mood. The revelers continue to jump one by one over the fire. One boy skids in the ash and falls on his hip, darkening his khaki shorts. Cara returns to the circle where the glowing heat shimmers on mesmerized faces and stares into the fire. As a child she jumped with excitement. Later, as a teenager she stood and stared with her classmates and mocked those who participated. When she became an adult with a responsible job she observed with colleagues and maintained adult decorum, no longer able to be spontaneous and play. Together they criticized those who attempted to overcome the obstacle and land safely on the other side.

A space opens up and a man nudges her elbow signaling for her to take a turn. She gasps and stares wide-eyed at him to protest. Her legs feel limp, but she decides not to think too much. She clenches her fists, says a little prayer, and takes three running steps. Her right leg leads. The embers spread out in a three foot circle below her with logs that lean together in the center. As she soars through the air, the flames lick at her soles. It seems the fire is observing her like a sentient being with a face, and eyes, and arms that reach out to heat, and help, and purify. She often thought of it as an enemy to overcome, something to conquer, but tonight, it seems to eye her with friendliness and buoy her up. Smoke curls off of its arms and ashes fly into the air, elevated by its hot breath. It seems pleased with her, happy that she has decided to be happy.

It reaches up, suspends her and encourages her to leap high. She holds her breath and the instant stretches out into an eternity. The fire whispers to her to "go," "fly," "be free." It smiles up at her and then she lands like a cat, surefooted and secure beyond the embers and flames on the other side. Elation blossoms in her heart. It's a lightness that she has never known before. When she looks back into the fire, she sees it has taken all of her weighty past, the bad feelings, the pain, the guilt and attachments, and consumed them. They are gone.

A feeling of accomplishment, pride, and gratitude overcome her. She praises the fire and understands what it offers. Wanting more, she turns, crosses half way around to the other side and leaps again. The fire's arms push higher and nearly lick at her thighs. Her body tingles with excitement. Her cells pump full of energy. The fire drives away the numbness that has threatened to sneak in like a thief and steal her joy at the new life and adventures awaiting her. She celebrates that she no longer feels bound by what others want and expect of her. The cord which has bound her to Gale disintegrates to ash. A surge of energy leaps from the base of her spine into her head and burns through her mind. Liberated, she thinks. I am free. And she turns to see the final flecks of her weighty attachments dissolve in the embers. She waves at the fire and swears it waves back nostalgically. "Ssssee," it hisses. "Ssseeiize the day!" it crackles, to remind her that life burns strong and bright for only a fleeting moment.

"I will, yes," she says out of breath and waves again before disappearing into the darkness of a side street below the medieval towers toward the sea. The moon looks smaller and farther away now. A smile spreads across her face and she ambles along humming, a childhood tune tickling her lips. The sea breeze dances over her skin and her flesh protests with goose bumps. At midnight she arrives home and unlocks her door, showers and slips under the white sheets to sleep deeply.

***

At home Cara dreams. A river. Gale walks with her beside the rushing water. Next Cara stands alone and observes someone in a car on an island extending out into the water. Tidal waves like from an earthquake shake the small car and pieces of rock wash down the roaring river. Other people feel the waves too, but hold fast to the land, to trees, to rosary beads they hold in their hands. Cara cries out, but no noise escapes her mouth. She sees a woman in the car and reaches out to her. "No," she wants to say. But no one can hear. Her scream is silent. Their fingers nearly touch as she stretches over the water and almost endangers herself. Cara considers jumping in to save her, but the current is too strong and the black waves stirred up by the quake are too powerful. Cara's knees go weak and she collapses on the ground weeping.

Cara comes to with damp sea smells in the air, as if she is in the hull of an old ship voyaging across the sea. She finds her cheeks wet, stained with dream tears as real as waking tears. Her heart feels swollen with grief. She lies awake until the first light stretches miraculously around the blinds and yawns into the small room. She searches for the meaning of the dream and then falls back asleep.

At ten, a bang-banging in her head translates into a bang-banging on the door. What? Where? The feelings of grief return. "Just a minute," she says louder than usual, but still below a yell. The door bell rings in place of the banging. She straightens a new t-shirt, zips up her white jeans, and glances at her reflection in the hallway mirror. Her eyes are red and puffy from a bad sleep and tears. A dread clenches her heart and she would rather do most anything than open that door.

"Ciao Cara," Arielle says. She stands beside her father, Rod, who appears waxen and gray.

"Morning," Cara says surprised. Arielle clasps her father's hand tightly. "I thought you guys were off to Monte Carlo." Their silence and their strange demeanor make her shiver.

"Can we come in?" Rod asks, his voice steady, controlled. His dull, narrow eyes peer past her and she wonders why Gale found him so attractive and irreplaceable.

"Come on in." She leads them to the living room and opens the wooden blinds. The fire of the sun's rays pours in. "What a gorgeous day! Very apropos for the start of summer, don't you think? Could I get you a coffee or something?" Her hair stands up in the reflection in the mirror and she works to smooth it into place. They wait in the in-between space where no one talks. Rod's puffy eyes search out her own. The dream of the figure washed away in the river invades her mind again.

"I...we need to talk to you," he chokes.

Arielle continues. "It's mamma. She had an accident." She announces this as if it were any other event like eating breakfast, going to school, or watching a movie.

Cara leans against the wall. "Is she in the hospital? Does she need help?" She automatically picks up her car keys and prepares to go. Their stillness and inactivity worry her. "Let's go," Cara says. Her keys tremble in her hand.

"Go up and get some of your things, *ma chérie*," Rod says. Arielle obeys. When the door closes behind her, Rod's eyes water uncontrollably. "She jumped." Cara's hands make fists on her hips.

"No she didn't. I tried to get her to last night, but she refused."

"You what?" Rod says stunned.

"It was St. Jean's last night. Did she finally jump over the fire?" Cara suddenly feels sorry, and imagines Gale finally mustered the courage and fell in the flames. Maybe Cara goaded too much. A wave of guilt floods her.

"No," he hesitates then starts again. "This morning..." The words catch in his throat. His lungs seem too taut to fill with the air necessary to form the words. She grabs his shoulders and shakes him impatiently.

"What happened?"

His face, gray with stubble, turns to meet her stare. "From a bridge, an overpass."

"Oh my God." A gasp of breath escapes her lips. Cara's heart freezes with panic. "What hospital's she in? We've got to go." Cara rushes off in a frenzy to grab a jacket. But Rod stands there, immobile.

"She's at Saint Anne's," he says. Cara searches for her purse and dabs on some lipstick.

"I'm going to give her a talking to when I see her," Cara growls.

"I never dreamed she'd actually..."

"No, you don't understand," he interrupts. Cara stops short.

"Is she in a coma?" And then the fact strikes her like a brick at her head. And the dream comes rushing back. His eyes confirm her fear. "You're not serious. It's not possible," she says. He does not answer. Nausea sweeps through her gut and she wants to wretch. Rod offers no words in exchange. What do you say in the face of death, when the words have not yet hardened into reality but seem like some eventual possibility? Cara looks into Rod's eyes and he collapses into her arms.

"I never thought so either. How many times she threatened it, but I never imagined…" He regains composure. "It happened this morning at 8:30. She left me a message saying she couldn't sleep." Cara thinks of the shock of the pedestrians out for a morning drive to buy flowers or get a croissant when Gale's frail body landed at their feet. "She must've planned it for quite some time. Her letters are dated from weeks ago," he says.

"Any for me?" Cara asks, dreading the answer.

"They found one in her car blaming me." Tears form irregular stains on his tan polo shirt. Between sobs, he says, "I told Arielle she had an accident. To protect her."

"What if she finds out," Cara says. "She'll never trust you again." Rod turns guiltily away.

"I'm supposed to leave in a few days."

"You'll wait until after the funeral?" Rod says. She wants to say no, to go away immediately and pretend it didn't happen, to imagine that Gale will be there when she returns from Spain. "You need to grieve," Rod says. She crosses her arms over her chest. "Could you stay with Arielle while I take care of the arrangements? I promise I'll come back and pick her up later."

Cara reflects, resists, then says, "Fine."

"If Arielle asks, please don't tell her." Rod pleads. Cara says nothing.

"You're only withholding the truth because you feel guilty. You think Arielle will blame you because you left her mother."

"What would you do in my place?" He bends his head like a guilty dog.

"But it's not your fault. It's no one's fault," she says and repeats it to herself.

***

The solstice marked the longest day of the year. Not the longest day really, for all days are twenty four hours, but the day with the most light. After that everything seems to decline, to wane and wither except the infernal heat that grows until mid-August. But it is only illusion, Cara, reasons. The fire of the sun shines with the same constant brilliance all year long. Its waning depends upon the tilt of the earth as its axis leans closer or pulls farther away. The light we get depends on how much we move closer or pull away. The sun remains steady and free of blame.

She cleans the toilet, the sink and bathtub. They scheduled the funeral for today. And not wanting to linger in the empty house, Cara plans to take the flight to Barcelona early in the afternoon as soon as it's over. She scrubs angrily at the sides of the tub, around the edges, in the grout. For three days Cara has lived in a daze, packing her things automatically into her suitcases, trying to eat, to go on about life as if it would all be the same. But absence of Gale's footsteps over head, or her voice calling Arielle to dinner, or the sight of her sweater on the back of the couch make the house seem bigger and emptier. Denial, anger, guilt, remorse, acceptance, these are the steps of loss. Her tears rinse the ceramic. She wants to yell at Gale and protest. You're a cheater, she screams. Then she sees Gale's tearful eyes on that last night and wants to hold her until she is whole and alive again.

Cara sets her bags in the hallway. Gale's dark eyes smile out of a usually overlooked photograph. Funny how things that are always around are so easily ignored and taken for granted. Cara slips it off the wall, recalling their childhood days: the two of them holding hands; making mud pies; and serving tea in dainty porcelain cups. "No one can ever replace you," she whispers. The night of St. Jean's plays over and over in her thoughts. What could she have done differently to change the outcome? Once Gale said she felt so low she could throw herself under a train, but sometimes she said she could kill Rod too. Just mindless expressions like everyone uses. Cara never dreamed her sister would ever really act.

Arielle sleeps in the bedroom next to Cara's. Her silent weeping haunted the rooms last night, but Arielle worked hard to be cheery during the day. She pretends that somehow, things will magically return to a time when her mother will walk back in, make breakfast, and take her shopping for dainty dresses and sequined shoes. Cara sees traces of Gale in Arielle's face and softly touches her cheek.

"We need to get dressed, sweetie," she says. The funeral is set for ten, a good time, a time when most people really start their day, make phone calls, come up with creative ideas and work most productively. They on the other hand move sluggishly, not wanting the moment to arrive for the final goodbye. Cara wears a white dress as a tribute to death with a black bow in her hair. Asians wear white for funerals. White for purity, renewal, transformation, and light. Arielle dresses in a pair of jeans and a dirty t-shirt.

"You really want to go out like that?" Cara says gently when she appears at the breakfast table.

Arielle's eyes peer up wide and dark and she starts to cry. The reality of being in a motherless world has slowly set in. "Yes," she moans.

"Come on, sweetie, put on your nice blue blouse at least. It's for your mom." Cara holds Arielle by the shoulders and coaxes her back into the bedroom to the closet where some of her clothes hang and locates the top. Arielle acquiesces while Cara pulls off her t-shirt and helps her slip her arms into the shiny blue fabric and pinch the buttons closed.

"Why did momma leave me?" she begs to know. It is an accusation and Cara senses that the child already knows that her mother made a choice instead of having an accident. Cara sits on the edge of the bed and wraps Arielle's small trembling body in her arms. Life is so strange and incomprehensible, she thinks. "I guess we'll never really know," she says softly and hugs her closely.

***

At the church, Arielle sits on the pew between Cara and Rod. The church fills up until people spill out the back door. The priest says something about their father, how he left them recently, how it shocked Gale so. And sorrowful friends offer condolences and beg forgiveness for not having called more often or said the word that would have changed Gale's mind. Gale's photo sits on the closed casket until the undertakers move it aside with the woven mat of red and white roses. Six men carry the casket to the car.

Cara watches them go. Aunt Ursula stands beside her. "You're still planning to go?" she says.

"Yes, it was a promise I made to myself."

"What about Arielle?"

"She's going to America with her father for a while."

"That's where his girlfriend's from..." Aunt Ursula's mouth twists up in disapproval.

"I think it will be good for them to get away and start a new life," Cara says.

By the time they reach the crematorium, the crowd has thinned. The wooden casket emerges from the black hearse and men carry it up the steps, with Rod, Arielle, Cara, and a few others behind them. This is a private ceremony. Inside, Celtic harp music plays in the background, followed by Pachelbel's *Canon*. The soft night of the full moon and the summer solstice flood back to Cara in a wave: the scent of jasmine mingled with sea air; the sound of the bongos; the tongues of fire. The priest drones on, but Cara's mind stays back in that other, better moment, that memory of her sister still alive flaring with rage and vibrant life. The mumbling stops and the door of the cremation chamber opens automatically. The wooden casket sails in, seemingly of its own volition, like a boat on the sea, swallowed into a black, endless night.

The door comes down. They all sit in silence, and the flames appear in her mind's eye. St. Jean's fire welcomes Gale, chides her for denying life, and purifies her of her demons. It embraces her in its arms and renews her until her anger, depression, and blackness burn away and only her goodness remains. The fire smiles and welcomes her. It melts her like gold and transforms her into a new, shiny, pure jewel. When it is done, it holds out a golden package of shimmering days, of moonlit nights, of solstices, and fire jumping, and smiles, and untainted dreams that they once shared. It offers these to Cara. Cara grasps them like shining jewels. She grasps life fully in all its bitterness and beauty and pain and joy. She weeps and grits her teeth and offers up her anger and pain to the fire, which it gladly consumes, and then it is gone, burnt out like life itself. But before Cara gets up to leave, before she heads off for the plane, she hears the fire whisper in the stillness.

"Ssseize the day," it says and she is sure that somehow Gale hears it too.

"Yes," she whispers softly. "Yes, I will. Yes." She feels the joy beyond the heavy clouds of pain, and in her heart she knows that Gale feels it too.

Chapter 8
Anthony's Butterfly

Marisa stands at the corner and glances at her watch. It's nearly five-thirty on Friday evening and cars rush down Albert 1st Boulevard lined with plane trees. The light turns green and Marisa walks fast. Her high-heeled shoes click against the pavement. When she reaches the curb a man in front of her falls. He crumbles like an ancient tower. His beret flies from his hand. His bald head raps against the concrete. He lies on his back on the sidewalk, and his plaid, woolen jacket hangs down over one shoulder. Marisa stops, kneels. He looks up in a daze.

"Are you alright?" she says.

The man places his hand against the concrete and sits up slowly. A caterpillar crawls by on the ground. "Look, a future butterfly," he says and Marisa looks at him, puzzled. He points to it, then kneels on one knee and pushes up on the other leg.

"Is anything broken?" she says. Her hand slips under the pit of his arm to steady him as he stands. His knees are shaky. His six foot frame, hovers over the three others who've stopped – a young woman with a baby in a carriage, an old woman with pale lavender hair who shakes her head sadly, and a teenager on roller blades with a walkman plugged in his ears. "I don't know what happened," the old man says.

Marisa scans the little crowd. They seem disappointed that there is no drama, and they roll, hobble, and skate away. "Shall I call an ambulance or a doctor maybe?" she says. He reminds her of her grandfather who once held her on his knee.

"I'm fine now. I'll be on my way." She picks up his plaid beret from the pavement and hands it to him. He puts it on and starts to walk away, but his legs tremble. She walks beside him a few feet to a green park bench. He sits. "I'm fine, really," he says. "I fell last week too. It's getting to be a bad habit."

"Where do you live?" He points with his cane down the block.

"Over there," he says.

A middle-aged man stops. "Ah, Monsieur Ponts," he says. "How are you?" Monsieur Ponts tells him about his accident.

Marisa excuses herself and walks away. She automatically touches the book bag hanging over her shoulder and feels the pile of homework expecting grades. What's left to prepare for class Monday? The handouts are bound and ready to go out, and the lecture on Molière is as familiar and automatic to her as the daily drive to high school. Oh, and for dinner, buy tomatoes and mozzarella with fresh basil if they have it. She walks toward the grocery, past Antibes' harbor, absorbed in the memory of fresh basil leaves crushed between her fingers.

***

The low hum of a plane eases out the edge of the afternoon as it fades into evening. Marisa walks to her apartment, her arms filled with groceries. A freshly baked brown bread, eggs, tomatoes, and early strawberries with their sweet smell, just like the ones she used to eat fresh from the patch as a kid. The slow setting sun reminds her the days are longer, and the slight breeze carries the scent of acacia flowers that dangle from the trees. The sky above turns a golden pink and the streets seem at rest before the tourists arrive in a few weeks. Monsieur Ponts is still there on the green bench. The pigeons coo and strut near his feet. He stands. Unsteady. She smiles at him. Something touches her. Maybe it is the light in his eyes, or that lost look as if the world is racing by and he doesn't know how to step into the whole whirling, spinning race again without being knocked over. It brings her to stop.

"Are you heading home?" she says. He nods; a look of relief relaxes the muscles in his worn face.

"It's the Residence Azure," he says. He anchors his cane on the sidewalk, stretches the fingers on his hand and grips the cane. His fingers are thick and powerful, like a ploughman's hands. They seem to ache to close tightly around the handle.

"It's in my direction." She sees he is a proud man, a big man, and does not take him by the elbow. But she shifts the groceries unconsciously to her other side leaving the hand nearest him free. He carefully maneuvers the cane, and his big feet slide one after the other toward home. Occasionally, he wavers and Marisa reaches out her hand near his back, but he steadies himself against the stone wall that runs along the sidewalk. In ten minutes, they walk the one small block to the residence. Monsieur Ponts tips his hat.

"Good evening," he says.

"You too," Marisa says smiling. Usually the groceries would be weighing her down about now, but she feels light and content. She unlocks the door to her building and hums as she steps into the elevator. When she unlocks the door to her apartment the heavy silence and solitude rush to surround her. Her home and her heart feel empty and she turns on the TV to let the comforting noise of human voices fill the space. But just for an instant, the instant with Monsieur Ponts, she had forgotten herself and the weight of her solitude had fallen away.

***

It's Saturday morning and the scent of hot coffee tickles her nose as Marisa walks down the stairs of her apartment building. No class today, no teaching, and she wonders what she will do. Last night she swept the floors. All her lesson plans are prepared for the next two weeks and she feels the uneasy nagging of aloneness that creeps in when the work is caught up and the days are sweet and sunny outside. This morning she carries her woven basket to the covered fruit and vegetable market in Antibes' old town. She doesn't really need anything, but it will be nice to hear the voices of the vendors selling their "eggs from happy chickens" and roses from the Cap d'Antibes' last greenhouses.

From a few feet away, she sees Monsieur Ponts sitting on the bench in front of his building. His forehead is crinkled. His head jerks around at the sound of the door opening. A woman with a child buzzes at the door. A mockingbird on the electrical wire above him sings joyfully, but he watches the people and his forehead crinkles more.

"Good morning. You're looking fine today," Marisa says. He squints at her, then smiles.

"Yes. I suppose so. It's easier for you. You're still young."

She sits down beside him. "You're feeling well?" she says.

"As good as can be expected. At my age, you know…"

"Have you lived in Antibes long?"

"All my life. When I was your age, this was all sandy beach and parasol pines." He motions up and down the street covered with four-story apartment buildings. The door opens and he looks over her shoulder. "That's the manager of the residence. They all leave early on Saturday," he says anxiously. Women in white uniforms file out giggling and chatting gaily.

"You have family?"

"My son lives in upper Antibes, near the technology park. He's a very busy man." He looks at his watch. "My travel show's on soon," he says and stands. Marisa accompanies him to the door.

"What's your name?"

"I'm Marisa Gardes."

"Anthony Ponts. Nice to meet you."

***

It's Saturday again, and several weeks have passed since she last saw Anthony Ponts. Marisa buzzes the guardian of the Residence Azure. This time she carries a pot of pink azaleas wrapped in newspaper from the market. The guardian peers through the glass door and opens it. The hospital-like silence of the residence envelops her with a sense of security and calm.

"I'd like to know about Monsieur Ponts. Is he doing okay?" she says. The guardian's face softens and he looks at her spring flowers.

"He fell again yesterday. You can go up and see him."

"I don't want to impose."

"He doesn't have many visitors. It'll do him good. T-9, third floor." He points to the elevator. She waits in front of it. Once it arrives, it rides up the floors with a slow, even gait, like a tame, old horse attentive to a young child riding delicately on its back. Its pace is slow, steady, even, without jerks or starts. The doors glide open with the same steady, even pace. She walks down the corridor lined with wooden hand rails. The walls are painted pale peach. T-9. The door is open. The sound of the television fills the hallway with jingles from commercials. His name is under the buzzer. She rings.

"Come in."

"Monsieur Ponts? It's Marisa." She walks in. He sits on a recliner, his foot up on a kitchen chair, the remote control in his hand.

"Take a seat." He motions to her to take one from under the kitchen table.

"No, I can't stay. I hadn't seen you out in a while." It has only been a few weeks and outdoors the almond and cherry trees are full of new green buds and pink blossoms, exploding into bloom, growing bigger and bigger. But Anthony Ponts' frame is smaller, stooped, like time is washing it away and he is dissolving little by little into thin air.

"I fell again. That's life." His voice sounds choked and regretful when he speaks. "It'll be a few days before I can get out again." He tries to get up and winces.

"You hurt your back?" He nods and looks at the kitchen table, just out of reach.

"Could I get something for you?"

"The pack of cigarettes."

She hands him the pack with the lighter. He lights one and holds it between his thick fingers and coughs once at the first puff.

"They're not good for you," Marisa says gently.

"At my age it doesn't much matter anymore."

Marisa watches the cigarette burn down until a long grey ash hangs precariously on the end. She hands him the ashtray. His face looks drawn and anxious. "Do you need anything from the market?"

"They're bringing me lunch from downstairs. But I'll need some bread tomorrow."

Marisa smiles. "Good. I'll bring bread in the morning."

"The one with sesame seeds," he says. "Like that one on the table."

She moves toward the door. "See you tomorrow."

***

The next day, Sunday, the sky is dark grey and the seagulls circle inland laughing in that funny way they do when it's about to rain. Marisa carries the bread, still warm from the baker's oven to the Residence Azure. She feels purposeful and content, as if Monsieur Ponts' bread has filled her usually lonely Sunday with meaning and warmth. The guardian opens the door rubbing the sleep from his eyes.

"Good morning," Marisa says. "Hope I didn't wake you."

"No, no."

On the third floor, she buzzes at Anthony's door. It is closed. No response. She buzzes again. No answer. She turns the door knob and it clicks open.

"Mister Ponts," she says hoping not to wake him.

"Uh."

"Mister Ponts, I have your bread."

"Uh, uh." She peeks around the corner of the entrance, past the kitchen table, past the TV and easy chair. His bed is set off in an alcove. "Here, here." Around the corner, she sees feet and legs, long legs grown weak sprawled on the floor like a rag doll. He is face down on the cold tile floor. His arms struggle to lift him. "I can't get up." She kneels. Even with the withering and the wearing away of time, his frame is too heavy for Marisa to lift alone. She rests a hand gently on his shoulder.

"I'm going to get the guardian."

"Don't go. Call." He points to a buzzer a few feet away, just out of reach. Marisa pushes the buzzer and stays close to him, on her knees.

"We'll have you up in no time," she says.

***

When the guardian leaves, she sits beside his bed watching the swallows zip past the window. They are dark, velvety blue and their underbellies flash glints of gold as they dash and dive swiftly through the air.

"It's truly spring. The first swallows are here," she says.

"Swallows are no proof it's spring. That's what the old-timers always used to say anyway," he says. He tilts his head and winks at her. She smiles. Out the window, the brilliant sun flows through the trees and the cloudless sky. Pillows prop him up. "Last time that happened, I crawled to the buzzer and called myself." They sit in silence, watching the sparrows.

"I love birds. They're always happy," Marisa says. Marisa glances at the walls and notices some butterflies pinned under frames hanging on the wall. Anthony notices her looking at them.

"There's one there too," Anthony says. "That's my favorite." He sits up and points to one across from them. It is a huge, greenish-blue one with spots in the center of the wings which look like big eyes. "When I look at them, I remember they were once ugly worms. And look what they became." A bitter look crosses his face. He leans back and reflects. "Maybe we're like them, like ugly worms waiting to be transformed into something better too." He draws his feet to the edge of the bed as if he wants to get up, but his knees shake from the least amount of pressure.

"Damn," Anthony says shaking his head. "You'd think there would be some sense to it all." Marisa sighs and sits beside him not knowing what to say. A thought nudges in, inches in, and then invades her mind. Someday, she too will grow old just like him. A sad, grey veil falls over her. But her stomach growls and a pang of hunger pulls her back to her comforting routine.

"It's almost lunch time. I left the bread on the table wrapped in a towel so it stays fresh," she says finally. "It's the one with the sesame seeds."

"How much do I owe you?" Anthony asks.

"Oh, nothing."

"I'm making filet mignon in a cream mushroom sauce for lunch."

"You cook?" Marisa says surprised.

"My wife's been gone for seven years."

"You enjoy it?"

"I'm baking apples too. I like to go out too. You know that Chinese restaurant on the corner? When my back's better, we'll go there." She stands to go. He looks at the clock on the wall. It's nearly noon. He hangs his feet over the edge of the bed and sits up. "I'm going to start lunch. On the weekends we have to cook for ourselves. The rest of the time they get lunch for us."

"You need a hand?" Marisa says.

"No. My son's coming." She leans over and kisses him on both cheeks the way she did with her father. His face is prickly from the beard growth. The blue veins in his face are visible through the skin.

"Okay. I'll drop by soon."

***

It's Sunday again, a week later. It's one of those brilliant sunny days when the light looks like crystal on the snow-peaked mountain tops in the distance, and the sea sparkles with finite diamonds on its smooth surface. It is a day to go out. Not anywhere in particular, just out, to stretch legs, to breathe the air, to feel alive, to hike through a mountain pasture with a lover. But Marisa promised to visit Anthony and she sits by his easy chair in the semi-darkness. His shutters are only partially opened. The lights are out and the TV is off. Water trickles in the fountain in the courtyard and the notes of a piano lilt through the window and lift the curtains on a light breeze.

"That's Ida playing," he says. A soft, nostalgic tune floats around them filling Marisa with a yearning for some distant, protected childhood place that exists only in her imagination. "It's against regulations. So she plays softly," Anthony adds. "She used to make records." His legs are propped up on the kitchen chair and he relaxes in the leather recliner. The white smoke of his cigarette curls up and over his head like a little halo. His shoulders are drawn forward. His legs are thinner. The skin on his arms is loose where the muscle has worn away. His pajamas lay over the back of a chair, and his usually neat room is scattered with a day old newspaper, a TV guide, some magazines his son brought, and the table is stacked with prescriptions and boxes of pills.

"The doctor came yesterday," he says. "He says there's nothing wrong with me. My blood pressure's fine. My heart's in great shape." He shrugs his shoulders and lifts his eyebrows. A grey shadow passes over his face. Marisa reaches out and lightly touches his arm.

"You feel okay?" He takes out his hearing aid and adjusts the volume. She hears its high-pitched whine.

"It's this back. Hand me that box there." He points to a pill box on the table, one with green writing on it. He punches two pills out of their foil and pops them in his mouth.

"I'll get some water," she says. He stubs out the cigarette and grasps the armrest with the other hand. Marisa hands Anthony the glass, a bit too full. His hand trembles as he lifts it to his lips and water spills down the front of his loosely buttoned shirt. He points to a cloth napkin on the table and Marisa hands it to him. He dabs away the water on his chest. Anthony turns to her and tilts his head. His face lights up.

"I'm ready for a walk." He takes hold of his cane and points with disdain at a metal four-legged contraption. "The manager wants me to use this, but it's awful." He struggles once, twice, three times to get up. She stands in front of him, her feet anchored against his. He grips her hands and in one heave she pulls him to his feet. Only now, when he stands, he is stooped and shorter, as if he shrank, like a wool sweater she once put in a dryer. Where does it go, she wonders.

They take the elevator up this time, to the terrace with a view of the deep blue sea. The breeze is cool and the sun warms their heads. Anthony walks to the edge of the terrace.

"It's the first I've been out all week," he says. He holds onto her shoulder just an instant to steady himself while he moves the cane to the other hand.

"It's a beautiful day," Marisa says. She stands behind him now, ready to steady him if he wavers. The stooped figure gazes silently at the horizon and for an instant, she sees his withered hand on the cane and studies her own hand. It is soft, smooth. The fingers move easily and smoothly and yet his hand was once like hers, perfect and agile. A pain pierces her heart and suddenly she sees herself in the inevitable pull of life toward that withered end. Odd she thinks, how we study to learn a language or to build computers, but no one ever teaches us about the most important things in life, like how to love, where to find happiness, or how to die.

She stands there beside him wanting to ease his suffering, wanting to say something profound that will make his withering away less tragic and sorrowful. But all the words that come into her head fail to bridge the gap that separates one human being from another.

They stand there looking out at the sea and the little boats bobbing toward the infinite horizon. He turns and their eyes connect a long moment. He nods as if he understands her heart, then he begins his slow shuffle toward the door. She feels the warmth between them and for an instant she wants to sob, then she catches herself and stares at the sea a moment before turning to follow him inside.

When they return to his apartment, Marisa helps him to settle in and prepares to go.

"Papa," a voice calls from the hallway. "You there?"

"My son," Anthony says. A man about fifty years old with thinning brown hair and a round face pokes his head past the doorway. His face registers surprise at the sight of Marisa.

"I thought the staff was off today," he says to Anthony.

"I'm not part of the staff," she says.

"This is Marisa," Anthony says. "She lives around the corner." His son lifts a hand and waves uncomfortably as if trying to wave her away.

"I'm just on my way out," Marisa says. "Goodbye, Monsieur Ponts." His son accompanies her to the door and looks at her suspiciously.

"You won't find any money here," his son says as they stand at the threshold.

Marisa stares back at him an instant perplexed, then she recalls the *Nice Matin* stories about people scamming the elderly. "We help each other," she says hoping to reassure him.

The son shakes his head as if this is impossible between an eighty-year-old man and a woman of thirty. "Help each other," he says with a snort of contempt. "Don't you have your own family?" he says. "Or a husband or friends to see?" She stares back at him in silence, but does not reply. His face wrinkles with disapproval. Marisa watches suspicious thoughts run past his eyes – how he considers she might be a thief or hope to get in his will or god knows what else. She turns away and steps into the hall, and then turns back to face him.

"It may sound strange to you, but we're friends."

***

It is Sunday again, another week gone by. The staff have all gone and only the guardian is there to open the door. She carries *muguet* flowers and a pink rose. He sticks his nose in them and inhales deeply.

"So nice," he says. She hands him a branch of the white *muguet* that looks like a row of little white bells. He smiles and holds the door open for her. "He can't stay, you know. We don't have the means to look after him. Maybe you can talk to him." Marisa's smile fades. Her face is placid like a still lake.

"Did he fall again?"

"No. But he's weak. As long as they're in good health and independent, but…"

"I see."

The elevator lifts her up to the third floor, stops gently and the doors open quietly. His door is open. She hears his TV. She suspects he leaves the door open so someone will hear him cry for help if he falls. Today he sits in his armchair. She sees his nearly hairless head from behind and it reminds her of a featherless baby bird. She knocks loudly.

"Wait, wait," he says anxiously. She returns to the hallway and waits for several minutes in the dark. "Okay," he says in a raspy voice. He sits in the easy chair wearing blue sweatpants and no shirt. "I was naked as a worm. It's this heat." She blushes and kisses him once on each cheek, then shows him the flowers.

"It's for May Day. I'll put them in some water." The cabinet doors stand open and she finds a tall mustard glass and fills it. "Nothing." He shuts off the TV. "Nothing. No soccer. No travel."

"You sleep well?"

"I always sleep well." He points to the framed butterflies by his bed. "I dreamed about them last night. I was in a cocoon of light and it was about to break open," he says excitedly. "But I woke up before the end."

She moves the kitchen chair beside him, next to the window. "What do you think it means?"

He shrugs. "Just a dream, I guess." His walker stands by his chair, and next to his bed is a plastic bedpan with urine in it. The bed is unmade and the remains of his breakfast, flakes of croissants, drops of jam, and coffee stain the tablecloth. Some crumbs cling to his chest. He sighs and shrugs.

"You go for a walk yesterday?"

"No. But I need to walk. I need to keep these muscles working." He sighs. His cheeks are hollowed and his eyes have sunken deeper into his head. "Go to that drawer over there." He waves his long finger toward a buffet with a porcelain bowl on top.

"This one?" She opens it. It holds a pile of photographs.

"Bring them here." She hands them to him. "This is my wedding." He holds out a sepia photo of a proud, tall man with dark hair, a distinguished tailored suit, and a crisp white shirt. He is the kind of man who Marisa would turn to look at on the street, proud and self-assured, but not haughty.

"What a handsome man!"

"And this one here." He hands her a photo of a barbecue in the vast garden of a stone villa. "This was my house. They sold it. When my wife died, I didn't need all the space. I couldn't keep it up." He is older here, maybe fifty, a bald spot beginning to spread on the back of his head. His wife is rounder. He is sterner. The villa looks like one of the expensive ones on the outskirts of town, prob-ably high on the hill overlooking the sea with a forest around. He must have been a businessman or a politician to have owned such a nice place, someone with an elevated social status, Marisa thinks.

"You like to eat, huh?" she says, not sharing her thoughts with him.

"I used to cook and have lots of guests. New creamed potatoes with fresh peas. Lamb with Provence herbs with Châteauneuf-du-pape wine. Sometimes the mayor and government ministers would come. But that's long past. Most of them are dead." Looking at the photos is like opening little windows to the past, catching glimpses of his life. "That's my car. It's gone too." He shrugs and Marisa does not know what to say. He is not sad. He speaks in a matter-of-fact way, like this is the way life is. Things come and go in the ebb and flow. She stares at his face, into his blue-grey eyes with little clouds in the pupils. His eyelashes are mostly gone and the wrinkles around his eyes have turned to deep gullies.

"I want to put an inscription on my tombstone as a warning to anyone who comes to mock me. 'You are what I was. I am what you'll be,'" he says. The room is silent now, except for the thick, heavy tick of the grandfather clock that marks out the passing sec-onds with each swing of the pendulum. The metallic tick, tick, tick breaks the air and falls on their ears like drops of lead hitting the floor. Time passes. She watches him stare out the window, his face drawn in a silhouette. His chest moves up and down in an even breath. His breathing fills the silence and her breath unconsciously falls into rhythm with his. The veins in his neck throb with the pulse of life, beating out the rhythm of his heart. He turns and looks at her again, this time his eyes are softer and a drop of wa-ter glistens in one corner. The quiet shadows of the room contrast sharply with the stark light beyond the shutters that stand half open. She puts her hand lightly on top of his.

"What do you think happens?" he says. She realizes he is refer-
ring to death, reflects an instant, and weighs her words carefully.

"Hum," she says. "I don't know. Don't think much about it
really." She looks up at Anthony's framed butterflies. "I imagine
it's like them," she says pointing. "The worm transforms in the
cocoon. When it's over, a butterfly emerges. The worm part falls
away – and I suppose it dies, so to speak. But unless that old part is
left behind, a butterfly can't emerge in its place. They're really one
and the same though. The worm is gone. But it hasn't died, it only
transforms into something else, something beautiful and free."

"Like it changes clothes," he says.

"Something like that." Marisa says. He reflects and stares up at
the butterflies mounted in the frames.

"I like that. I can live with that."

***

Chinese carry out is on the menu today. Anthony wanted to go
out for lunch this Sunday, but his legs won't carry him, so Marisa
brings lunch inside. When she gets there, he has already set the
table with chopsticks, linen napkins and mustard glasses for the
bottle of Beaujolais which his son brought.

"Shrimp with curry sauce and ginger, and egg rolls and egg
fried rice," she says, emptying the contents of the bag one by one.
He sits there like an excited kid, his napkin on his lap, waiting for
her to serve him. He wears a fresh, white shirt with buttons and
today his stiff fingers must have miraculously cooperated because
the buttons are closed. His chin is nicked in several places where
the razor cut in, but he is clean-shaven and proud of it. His shaving
mirror sits on the table.

"You know it's usually just the two of us for meals," he says
jovially pointing at the mirror. "Me and him. It's nice to see another

face." Marisa smiles, content at the small joy the meal gives him. They take their time and he even manages to use the chopsticks with prowess. Some days he has miraculous moments of strength, and his will to keep going seems to overcome the increasing inertia of his muscles. Maybe he will make it through to summer.

"Papa," his son's voice resounds from the doorway. "Papa?"

"*Oui, mon cheri,*" Anthony calls out to him. His son walks to the table and leans over, embarrassed and awkward it seems, to kiss his father on the cheek in front of Marisa. "We're having a feast." Anthony booms and points at the open cartons of carry-out spread out on the table. "But we've just about polished it all off."

"We've got a lot of fried rice left over if you'd like some," Marisa says. His son's eyebrows rise in surprise as he looks back and forth between Marisa, Anthony and the cartons.

"No thanks, I've already eaten," he says.

"It was like a party!" Anthony's voice is jovial and light.

Marisa stands up to leave her seat for his son and quickly clears away the empty cartons.

"Who bought it?" his son says. Anthony jerks an accusing thumb at Marisa.

"I offered to pay for it, but she's stubborn. Just like a woman," Anthony grumbles, the tone of his voice hides his delight.

"I'll put these in the fridge and go," Marisa says. She shuts the remaining fried rice and shrimp cartons and puts them away, then leans over to kiss Anthony on the cheek. "Stay out of trouble," she says. He smiles and waves. She walks rapidly to the door hoping to avoid Anthony's son, but he follows on her heels.

"About the other day," he says speaking to her back. "I...I." She stops and waits for him to finish, but does not turn around. "Lots of work pressure, you know." His voice is apologetic. "He told me about you. About the fall. About the bread you bring, and how you took his hearing-aid out for new batteries but refuse to accept anything in return."

She twists her head and catches his eye. "It's natural to worry about him. You never know how much longer he'll be around. Goodbye, Mr. Ponts." She speaks softly and lifts a hand to wave goodbye as she steps out the door.

***

It is mid-week and when she enters his room, the housekeepers are there tidying and chatting.

"Monsieur Ponts is our darling," one says. She has red colored hair and a mole at the corner of her mouth. A butterfly flies past her and she bats it away. "They've been everywhere today. I wonder where they're all coming from?"

He lies on his bed, propped up by the pillows, wearing boxer shorts and his stripped blue pajama top. "Huh?" Anthony says.

"Put in your hearing aid," another woman says to him loudly, making a scolding gesture with her hand. "He can't hear without it," she says to Marisa. The woman walks to his bedside table, picks it up and thrusts it at him. He playfully holds his hand over his head like a school kid protecting himself from a teacher's disciplinary tap, and then he obediently puts it in his ear. He seems even smaller today, his feet gnarled up like an old, knotty tree branch. The soles are dirty. He notices Marisa looking at them and lifts one to inspect it.

"I hate to wear shoes," he says to her.

"We've finished," one of the housekeepers yells. "Have a good day." They wave and close the door behind them.

"How're you feeling today?" Marisa says. She grabs a kitchen chair and sets it by the bed.

"Tired." He struggles to sit up. "I'm just tired of it all. Even sitting up is a bother."

"I brought you some cakes. One with fresh strawberries and cream, the other is a baba with rum," she says cheerfully, hoping to change his mood.

"Take them back home with you," he says.

"But they're from your favorite bakery. You need to keep up your strength." He falls back into the pillows. His eyes roll up into the top of his head. Marisa holds her breath and reaches for the pulse in his arm.

His eyelids flutter and open again. "I won't be needing them," he says.

"Oh," she says and wants to run away. "Should I leave?"

"No. I was waiting for you." She looks into his eyes with concern. They look brilliant and full of light, almost out of focus, as if he stands on a threshold staring through her into another dimension. "I dreamed of them again," Anthony says pointing to the butterflies on the wall.

"What did you see?" She holds his limp hand.

"I left my cocoon. It was wonderful. I didn't want to wake up."

"Oh," Marisa says in a muted voice. Goose bumps travel up her arm, send a shiver up her spine.

"I think you're right about the way it works."

Some tears glimmer in the corner of her eyes. Her forehead wrinkles. "I'll come back to see you tomorrow," she whispers. A deep silence surrounds them. The clock ticks heavily. Anthony's breathing becomes labored.

"Let me call a doctor," she says. "Or the guardian. I've got to go," she says, but she doesn't move. Anthony shakes his head no. His eyes sparkle with a distant serenity, as if he is about to embark on a long and comfortable voyage. Marisa tenses, sits on the edge of her seat. She wants to run away. But Anthony grips her hand

and she waits expectantly. A soft light surrounds them. Anthony's eyes flutter, and a rattle emerges from his chest, as if something has been loosened and set free. Finally, his fingers relax and his hand goes limp in hers. She sits there in the silence and shakes him anxiously, but he does not respond. For a moment she wants to panic, to flee in fright. She looks around helplessly, fully aware that he has left his cocoon. Where did that light, airy, invisible stuff of life go? She wants to know, wants to run after it, recapture it, put it back in and hold it there to make his heart beat again.

But the panic subsides and the room fills with a soft light. Instead of fear and dread, her heart fills with a deep sense of peace and contentment. Anthony's hand cools on her warm palm. She carefully leans over and kisses him tenderly on the cheek. Then placing her fingertips on his eyelids, she closes them shut. Her tears fall and they mix grief of losing Anthony with the joy of feeling the certainty that there is something more, something beyond this physical life. She detects a movement by the window. A butterfly enters, flies above her head, lilts lightly up and down. She watches it and remembers Anthony's dreams. The butterfly dances around her one last time, like a reflection of his soul, and darts toward the window out into the fading light.

Chapter 9
Mystical Sea

From the beginning of Halan's time, there was always the sea. He felt he was born from the sea and he found his solace in her. He dived for amphorae and found them strung along her sea bottom – amid the remnants of some sunken Greek ship that sailed from Antipolis with wines and olive oil two millennia ago. Only once did he find a perfect one, still filled and sealed, and he swam back to the shore with it. But out of the water, it looked taciturn and the barnacles began to turn a deathly gray, so the next day, he took it back and deposited it among the fragments of dreamy red pottery thirty-one meters beneath the water's surface.

He lived on a little island off of the coast of Cannes – the one where legend says they held the Man with the Iron Mask. As a child Halan had played in the dungeon there with bars on the windows, but the doors stood wide open now for tourists and kids and dogs to ramble in and gawk or imagine or pee in a corner. The man with the mask, from King Louis' time, haunted his dreams and begged to be set free. When Halan walked inside the dungeon, he could still hear the whimpers of the tragic figure – face hidden behind

iron to keep others from knowing his identity – pleading and cursing with his brother, the jealous king who had placed him there to
protect his sovereignty. A victim of circumstance, of unfortunate
birth, of choosing the wrong mother at an inopportune time.

Halan's family kept a small boat to travel to and from the main-
land. They hated to depend on anyone – especially the ferry to take
them at specified hours. So he possessed no car (no one did on the
island), but he owned a small motor boat to carry him to the bigger land half an hour away. Each time he found himself seated by
the motor with an errand to run in Cannes, his eyes would turn
away from the polluted coast out to the borderless horizon. He felt
a strong urge to set out for deeper sea.

Sometimes his mother made him ferry her over to Sunday
morning mass on the tiny St. Honorat Island just behind theirs.
A small group of monks wearing white hassocks over black robes
owned and peopled the place. They spent their days chanting ves-
pers, fondling rosaries, and tending their vines while peacocks
strutted through their vineyards. Tiny men, aging men, sexless
men with passions for God and wine. The sound of the abbey's
bells echoed through the sea when he dived below the surface, vi-
brating and rushing through the waters.

In his silent lingering, he learned the lessons of the sea; how
to love it in its entirety; how to embrace it with more than just his
arms; how to become one with it and lose his identity. This was
the best gift, the sweetest gift it offered – the possibility of merging into it, and losing himself, and then suddenly realizing he was
everything. His mom once accused him of being more monk-like
than those habited men across the way, but he lowered his eyes
and said nothing as usual and looked out to her, to the sea. With
the sea as his lover, he could never be only for some distant God
painted on ceilings and walls like they professed to be.

On one balmy spring as he carried his air tanks to the sandy shore, a woman appeared, alone, distraught. She sat on the sandy beach by the pier. She wasn't like the tourists who gawk at him and the island as if they are in a zoo. Her long reddish-brown hair hung thick like straw, and her shoulders rolled inward; her head sloped down. He wondered if someone close to her had died. He fit his air tanks for scuba diving snuggly into the bow of the boat and he broke the silence of the gentle waves and squawking gulls by starting the motor. The woman didn't even turn to look. It seemed she was numb to life. Halan's wooden boat putted out to sea where he dropped anchor, strapped on the tanks and slipped backwards over the side of the blue hull. Once in the water, he flicked his flippers with a slight shift of the ankle and propelled himself ten meters down. He turned onto his back and looked up to see the sun stream through the water as the sea undulated and moved through the sea grass like wind.

Some curious fish, mostly finger-sized *girelles* with green and orange stripes, darted around him opening their round mouths. A cloud of small fish swam above him and they glinted like silver as they flicked onto their sides and reflected the sun. A trumpet fish darted through the grass, long and narrow like a piece of sea grass, and some transparent jellyfish floated on the surface shimmering pink and iridescent. He descended deeper into the blue water until the sea life disappeared. In that moment, suspended between the surface and the seabed, he saw only blue, a blue that went on forever it seemed. Blue extended in front, above, and below him. In his dreamy dive, this point with no references where he floated surrounded all in blue, he felt immensely alone, even though he knew that his lover, the sea was all around him. It still felt as if he were the only being in existence. Even the fish deserted him in this in-between space. He imagined that this must be the way the monks felt about God. Their omniscient God permeates all, and yet they seek Him and yearn for Him because they feel cut off and alone.

Halan held his breath, then watched the bubbles float out of his mouth and drift toward the surface. As he continued to descend, the relief of the sea floor came into view. Sometimes he tested his limits. In between the islands, the sea map told him that the floor plunged to some 2000 meters in depth. Sometimes the fishermen netted a pilgrim shark, the big, slow creatures that live at those depths and feed only on plankton. He wanted to go there, wanted to know what it would be like so deep in the sea's arms. The light faded at 40 meters and the sea turned into a vast, unfamiliar place. Day turned to dusk. The waters turned chilly, and spiny rock fish with flat heads stirred. A sharp-toothed Moreno eel as thick as his forearm darted out at him from a sea wall hoping to find lunch. With a flick of his flipper he undulated aside and avoided its poisonous bite. The bubbles from his breath floated in long wide trails to the surface. He dived down eighty, ninety meters, one-hundred and ten meters and found the corals his father had once harvested. It was red, stinging coral that they collected for jewelry and amulets before he was born. He went down alone to see, to know again what the pressure of her embrace felt like, to see if he could withstand.

He continued to slip through the arms of his lover, the sea, down into her darkness, until he saw a rock jutting up like the peak of a mountain, where some fan coral reached gloriously upward. When he reached out to pluck the beautiful thing, he found himself in a stupor, drunken and giddy from the pressure. Before he lost consciousness he saw a plane on the sea floor with its carcass broken into three parts and the reddish brown haired woman from the dock lay on the sea floor with her baby. He'd not seen the crash and yet he saw a woman dressed in a white gown swim toward the woman from the dock who held her baby nestled tightly in her arms. The mysterious woman in white lifted them both up from the ocean floor. Then she swam to Halan, took him gently by the arm, and she carried them all three up to the light.

When he awoke and looked at his diving gauge, he was alone and he realized he had lost consciousness as he sometimes did on deep dives. But she had carried him up to 70 meters instead of down deeper. The sea had been merciful this time. She had helped him make it back to the surface. His heart raced and he went through the decompression steps thankful for each new breath of life. When he perceived the boat's anchor and chain, he relaxed and realized his luck, how he could have died in her arms, but how she had freed him instead. He pulled off the air tanks and heaved his body onto the boat, then laid there in the sun for a long time staring up at the sky, as the boat rocked gently on the waves.

When the sun leaned heavily toward the red Esterel Mountains, he finally started the motor and returned to the shore more vibrant and alive. When death has been so near, life tastes sweeter and better than before. The woman sat there again on the sandy beach by the port staring into the water as if she were not there. He usually let things be, but he had seen her often recently and knew it must be getting late – too late for the ferry, and so he looked into her face – a pretty face with blue-green eyes that reflected back the sea. She turned to him and stared at the weighty tanks over one shoulder, and his wet suit smelling of neoprene and brine, and she said, "What?"

She was the woman from his sub-sea dream. "Have you missed the ferry?"

"Oh, that." It was as if she spoke through water – thick, slow. Maybe a mermaid would talk that way.

"Do you have no place to go?" He studied her face – full of youth, full of the sense of immortality, full of resignation to death, full of contradictions. She wore a white button down shirt over a pea-green tank top and white shorts. Her legs looked narrow and her feet seemed too big for her frame. Bony and narrow with straw-like hair. A pretty yet vacant stare.

She shrugged and turned back to the sea. "This feels like home."

She had been sitting there when he left, and seemed not to have moved from the spot all day. She lay down on her back and looked up at the sky where a cloud formed in her eyes. A tear formed too, but she smiled it away.

The ferry distanced itself from the island forming temporary watery mountains at the stern where the motor gurgled. "You've missed the last boat."

She seemed not to care. Her face held onto the smile; the tear fell down her cheek. "Oh well," she sighed.

"My mother will fix us something to eat. Then I'll take you back." He held out a hand and she stared back puzzled as if it were a foreign object, then her mouth formed an O. She gave him her hand and he pulled her to her feet.

Are you okay? He wanted to ask, but knew better. Something told him she wasn't and hadn't been for a while. She held onto the remnants of some shock; some tragedy lurked inside of her, but like the sea, she would spit up the refuse when she was ready and not before. Nothing could be forced.

"I had a dream just while I was sitting there." She pointed to the spot on the sand where the imprint of her narrow shoulders and round buttocks remained. "I saw a diver lose consciousness and begin to sink to the bottom."

"I saw you with a baby," he said.

She looked at him wide-eyed. "You saw my baby?" Some tears rose from her eyes.

"Another woman, the sea, she saved us," he continued. Her mouth opened as if she were about to say "Yes," yet no sound came out. She looked at Halan with water dripping from the sleeves of his black neoprene suit. Some green sea grass clung to his shoulder.

"I dreamed it too. But maybe it wasn't a dream."

"My," she sighed. The thought that someone else could share her dreams shook her out of her numbed stupor. "Maybe there is something more than what our physical eyes can see?" She wanted it to be a statement it seemed, but the words came out as a question.

He just shrugged. "It's no mystery really. It came from the sea. She does that to me."

"But what does it mean?" the young woman said. "It makes no sense."

"She gave back to you what you lost." The woman stared at him with a look of uncertainty. Halan did not know the meaning of the look in her eyes. She looked lost, frightened, and alone.

"You stared at her for a long time. Did you dive into her too?"

Her eyes look confused. "The sea, you mean?"

He looked back as if to say, 'is there anything else?'

"No, but I'd like to. It scares me though. You never know what you'll find."

"I suppose the unknown scares most people," he replied thoughtfully. "But she has been good to me."

They walked along in silence down the eucalyptus-lined path, under the dense growth of the island in the shadows of the late afternoon. Halan's feet were bare; he carried his long flippers hooked in his index and middle fingers. A cool, soothing eucalyptus scent stirred through the air as fallen leaves crushed beneath their feet.

"What do you find?" She turned to him with her big, curious eyes glowing like a cat's.

"Coral, amphorae, broken ships, lost anchors, red star fish." He paused as a breeze stirred the leaves and the scent of sea and salt danced through the air. He filled his lungs with it. "I almost found death. It waits there too, down deep. And dreams. And..." He turned to look at her. "Today, I found you there too."

She wrinkled her eyebrows together, unsure of what to say. "I guess I've got to get back to my work soon."

"What about your baby?"

"Oh that?" She placed her finger by her chin and pondered. "I held onto her so tight. I loved her so much in my dream. I swam fast to bring her to the surface and keep her alive."

"She's your soul," Halan says.

"I think I'd almost lost her," she says.

"Maybe you'd just misplaced her for a while."

"Yes," she reflected. "Like putting it in a closet and forgetting about it." The white wood-frame house came into view. It had small windows, a simple porch, and was nothing more than a cottage really.

"Mamma," Halan called out with a loud, but soft voice. "Set an extra plate for dinner. I've brought someone home." His mother, a dark-haired woman with a thin face and bright eyes peeked around the corner of the open door, waved, then disappeared.

"What did you bring home this time!" Her voice called from inside feigning irritation. Then she poked her head out again and sized up the woman standing next to Halan before disappearing one more time. Halan unzipped his wetsuit and peeled it off his chest and down over his shoulders, then sat down on the bench in front of the house to pull it from his legs and ankles. It hugged him snuggly like a black, slippery skin. The young woman watched him. His narrow chest had no hair yet and maybe never would.

"Do you know anything about the Man in the Iron Mask?" she asked. Her soft, oval face tilted at an angle.

"It's just a legend, some think." But he knew it was more. He stood up now wearing only a thin pair of tight swim trunks. The wet suit lay on the ground. It almost seemed he had shed an old skin. His flippers sat beside it.

"Everyone wears masks," he said. Sometimes in the fog, Halan thought he still saw the shadow of the young man wandering the island, trying to tear away the mask.

"But we're not forced to. He was. They say his brother, the king made him," she said. "That they locked the mask on his head so that no one would know his identity."

"Yes." He paused, then bent down to pick up his suit. She followed him to the back of the house where he threw it over a clothesline, rinsed it with a hose, and walked inside the back door. "This is my room." She followed close behind him to a space with bare wooden floors, driftwood, seashells, and faded print curtains with seagulls and ships on foamy waves. Whatever was outside, he had brought in so that it seemed that inside and out were one and the same.

"You love the sea," she said. He said nothing, but pulled a tan cotton sweater over his head and slipped on a pair of old jeans. She sat down on the edge of his bed. "What do you do?" She came from the land where to "do" meant to "be." His world was different.

"You judge a man by what he *does*?" He put special emphasis on *does*. She didn't answer. "I dive. Sometimes, when I need money, I bring back artifacts or coral to sell to merchants. But I don't need much, so I mostly leave them alone. I went for coral today."

"What do you need money for?"

"For the same reasons everybody else does. To eat, to pay bills, to buy my mother a new dress…"

"How much do you need? I can give you some." She reached into the bag on her hip and pulled out some bills, but he ignored her. When he wasn't looking, she slipped the money under the edge of a ship-in-a-bottle on his dresser. His mother's head appeared around the door again. This time she came into full view. She wore a worn floral print dress just over the knees, belted at the waist. Her dark hair was pulled into a bun. Her straight, white teeth seemed regularly parted in a smile, and her recessed eyes twinkled just enough to give her an impish look.

"Excuse me," she said, and looked back and forth between her son and the woman with the hope of a mother praying for grand-kids. "Soup's ready."

"Fish soup," Halan said. "It's the best. With *rouille* and croutons and pieces of rock fish. Funny how those things are poisonous if you put a hand on their spines yet you can eat them." The woman noticed that the hair on his arms stood on end. She wondered if he carried the chill of the sea still in him and reached out with her finger to touch his forearm. He pulled back as if she had given him an electrical jolt.

"I'm sorry," she said. "You're cold."

He ignored her, but rubbed his arms to heat himself. "Let's eat. I'm so hungry. The sea does that to me."

Halan walked inside the kitchen and the woman followed. Her feet shuffled over the worn floor boards. His mother motioned to a seat in a corner by a fireplace where some embers glowed. But the young woman's eyes caught on a porcelain doll perched on the mantel. It wore a white and blue lace dress. His mother lifted up the baby and handed it to the woman. Its porcelain feet clinked together. Its body was soft and cottony.

"It's very, very old," Halan's mother said. "So old it seems timeless."

The woman buried her face in its belly and then clasped it to her breast. Throughout dinner, she held it tightly, the soup spoon in one hand and the baby in the other. They ate to the sound of em-bers popping and spoons pinging against china bowls.

When they finished the meal, Halan led her to the boat. The motor churned out a regular low rhythm and he helped her step inside.

"You'll be returning to your family," he said.

"What family?" she grumbled. Then, she said, "Yes."

They passed the rest of the way in silence. The waves churned under the boat, the sun sank behind the red rock mountains, a dolphin swam by the bow of the boat and then disappeared. Life went on. Life lived itself. Life lived them. As he let her off at the dock in Cannes, he extended his hand to help her out of the boat. She said nothing and began to walk away. A vacant longing look played on her face as if she felt she should be somewhere else.

"Don't forget this," Halan called out behind her.

He handed her a crib-like basket and she retraced her steps carefully over the wooden dock. She reached down for it and found the porcelain doll inside. Her forehead wrinkled. She looked perplexed, then she reached out and accepted it. When she took it in her arms her face lit up and she clutched it tightly to her chest. Halan thought of the dream.

"Oh yes," she muttered and shook her head frustrated at her forgetfulness. Her tears formed and fell. "How could I forget?"

"Cling to her like you did in the dream, like you did over dinner."

"Yes, of course. I know that. I already know."

"Of course you do. The sea simply reminded you."

Halan loosened the ropes that bound the little boat to the dock and revved the motor. He raised his hand in a gentle, affectionate wave and the woman looked down at her baby, then back up to Halan and whispered, "Thanks." He set off and she followed the point of light that lit his prow until it disappeared into the night sea.

Chapter 10

Whispers of the Soul

Horses. Horses running wild this morning. I'm sitting on one's back, clinging to a man. Racing. Too fast. Danger of falling off, of falling down, of getting hurt. The horse is black, sleek, powerful. Out of control. Wind rushing through my hair – a feeling of excitement and fear. The wild rider veers. I fall. Hit my head. Black out. Come to with a start. Heavy breathing. I struggle to catch my breath. Paralyzed from fear, disoriented, I flip back the edge of the sheets and punch on the bedside light. A dream. Just a dream. I'm fine. Nothing's hurt. Not yet. I lie on my back looking up at the pink, hand-blown light fixture that looks like a nipple. The room glows pink and my breathing relaxes; my eyes adjust. It's the same familiar, comfortable surroundings – the Japanese screen prints of bamboo, the cherry-wood bed. I hear the soothing sound of the seagulls beyond the blind and I reach out for Jason, but he's gone.

Stupid dream. It gave me such a fright. Julie believes that it all has a meaning. Nothing happens by coincidence. Dreams are messages from the soul, she insists. But this is nonsense. Silly. Who's ever seen a soul anyway? It's probably just another one of those tribal myths we've carried over from our primitive past, one that we haven't yet outgrown. A comforting idea to hold onto like a life-jacket in distressing times. Besides, how can you relate to something that you cannot see? Julie's a little flaky; she has a guru too.

I flip off the light switch, but get out of bed. Too much adrenaline to sleep. Funny how some dreams do that to you. My legs feel shaky as if I just ran a sprint. But I never left my bed. It all happened in my mind. I push the button by the window to raise the electric blinds. The motor hums and dawn spreads out before me over the dark sea. Venus sparkles there at the edge of a new moon hanging out over the water like some crystal decoration from an expensive Swedish boutique on the rue d'Antibes in Cannes. Venus shimmers, calls out. I wonder what secret code it uses to communicate with me. The blue light in the sky grows lighter and the star dims. The sky turns a golden-pink. The sea does too, tinged with deep blue. The pink lip of the sun edges up out of the water as if it is born from the sea. The world turns.

In the kitchen, I flip on the espresso machine and open a box of muesli and pour some into a bowl. Add milk. The seat at the narrow counter is my favorite spot since Serge left. It's good to breakfast alone, to not have to face the back of his open newspaper and to fix his coffee. It gives me space and time to get to know myself, what I like, what I need. After nearly five years of compromise, of living with him and doing what he liked, of refusing to listen to my own heart, it's about time.

Horses. The mad stallion from the dream races through my mind while I stare into the bowl and count each spoonful and chew, one, two, three, all the way to thirty. The animal is sleek, perfect, strong and very dangerous when not kept under tight control. Once I begged and cried for a horse on my birthday. My father finally gave in and bought it for me. A dark horse with blond manes. Like in the dream, it was fiery, snorting nervously, moving its legs and hooves, whisking its long tail. When it took off it reared back on its hind legs and sprinted into the pasture. My father warned me it was dangerous, bigger than the ones I was used to. But I rode bareback by the white wood-frame house in Iowa, scared, but determined to master him.

But this is Antibes, thousands of miles away, in a foreign country. The only horses here are in the circus or on the equestrian farms at the foot of the mountains, or in the engines of powerful cars. Million dollar yachts float in the port unused most of the year, and tourists flock here to look enviously at the wealth while the thieves who arrive for the summer break car windows and grab purses, then buzz off through the bumper to bumper traffic on mopeds. It happens in town almost every day in the summer now. I see a lot of things that I never saw or imagined in Iowa. There, we left our car doors and houses unlocked and the neighbors watched for unfamiliar faces. Here, so many people come and go. Locked doors and distrust of strangers is the price to pay for anonymity.

When I open a new tin of freshly ground coffee, the warm delicious smell of Ethiopian Arabica brightens my day like a pink sunrise; it soothes me. In two scoops, a twist of the handle and a push of the black button, the espresso machine fills my cup. With the first sip, I finally calm down, relax into the day. The sun is up now, fully out of the water and its rays stream through the window. It's good to be alive – and not hurt or paralyzed or dead from a wild horse. A little later, I will go out for lunch and wait for Jason's return. It will be nice to sit in the sun.

***

I first met Jason in mid-May. It was nearly noon and the sun warmed the top of my head and ran its fingers down my back like the caress of a friendly hand. I walked down the long flight of stairs to the *Azure Plage* beach. The white rugged rocks leaned into the sea and a few parasol pines sheltered overweight, oily tourists who grilled sardines and drank cheap rosé on the ground. On the right, the restaurant was gearing up for the season and the waiter bobbed up to me and forced on a smile.

"*Bonjour*," he said and escorted me to a table a few meters from the water, my favorite spot. "Want a menu?"

I daydreamed about ordering a sole *munière* and a glass of champagne with strawberries and whipped cream for dessert. That's what I used to get when Serge was around, when I felt like a princess. But I made the mental calculation of the cost and thought about how long it might be before the settlement. That was when I believed in the myth of a Prince Charming. The story recurred often enough when I grew up that I imagined it could become a reality, that a man, not unlike my father, would take care of me and life would be easy. No pressure to make decisions or fail or make mistakes. Serge did that for me. Then he left. My emotional landscape of pretty pink dreams and happily-ever-after romance broke into shards of anger, confusion, and fear.

"I'll just have a *salade Niçoise* and a glass of rosé," I said and opened the *Herald-Tribune.* It was black-and-white boring and full of bad news, but it brought me closer to the U.S. This time as I read about the proliferation of video games and murders, it only made me feel more alienated from the fads and fashions back home, and from my parents who I talked to once a month on Skype. A sea breeze filled the air with the smell of sardines and pulled loose a page of my paper and blew it to the ground.

"I'll get it." A man with an English boarding school accent handed it to me. I wasn't sure I liked him. He was too smooth, too attractive with his golden-tanned hand whisking through his blond hair. The hair looked like the blond mane of the horse dad had bought. The one that threw me.

"*Voilà*," the waiter said and placed the salad on the table. I picked the anchovies out, nibbled at a radish and thought of diving below the water to look for shiny pearl-toned shells.

"Eating alone?" I heard the English accent again. I hate admitting to such an embarrassing fact. No, I'm eating with the ghost of my ancestors, I wanted to snap back.

"You're doing an anthropological study or something?" He jerked back, a little unsure, which seemed a rare sentiment for him.

"Why yes, I'm studying the customs of the French Riviera." His sarcasm matched mine. He had a cleft chin and high cheek bones like Clint Eastwood in his youth. Good skin and straight white teeth, too perfect and too white, and I wondered if he had ever had cosmetic surgery. "I find an uncanny resemblance between mating rituals in Juan-les-Pins and those of the aborigines in Papua New Guinea." He paused. His tone softened. "I'm sure a beautiful woman like you only dines alone because she wants to. You must be surrounded by men." He clasped his glass of gin and tonic. Beads of water rolled down the sides.

"One's enough, if he's the right one." Men! So pretentious. I'd been trying to live without one for the past six months, but frankly, I felt lonely. I'd rather be in love. But Julie said that I needed to clear the slate first before starting over; that Serge abandoning me was only symbolic of me abandoning myself. She reads too much Jung.

"There's only one way to find out if he's right..." His hand automatically flipped up the cuffs of his blue and white striped shirt as if he were getting down to some serious work. He looked quite striking and knew it; I wondered if I had seen him on TV or on the cover of the *Nice Matin,* the local paper that flaunted every pretty faced celebrity that arrived to sell more copies.

"And what would that be?" I softened and waited, glancing at him sideways.

His eyes squinted in amusement and his lips turned up slightly at the corners. "We'll get around to that later."

So cock-sure, I thought. "You must be from the U.K."

"From London."

"With all the cheap flights, you guys are flooding the place. Nice used to be quite nice."

His face twisted up. "We've got to give the French something to complain about."

The sailboats in the bay bobbed behind him, and a small child with a fish flapping on the end of a cane pole stood on the quay. Waves licked gently near my feet while the sun's warm rays massaged me like hands penetrating into my back. A sigh eased up from my lips and I half – closed my eyes like a cat in the sun. A few brilliant, white clouds puffed up against the azure background, and it seemed the sea and sky competed to display the deepest and most soulful shade of blue.

"I can hardly blame you or anyone else who flocks here. I love the *Côte d'Azur* too. The Blue Coast."

"Mind if I join you? You know what the French say, *les hommes proposent et les femmes disposent.*" His voice came out as a sexy whisper as if he were telling a secret. Men propose and women dispose, I repeated silently. Serge had said it often too, but in the end it had been the other way around.

"Ha, ha." I forced a chuckle, the kind that revealed the unease down below, then I turned to look at him straight on. He smiled and his tanned cheeks glowed. I daydreamed of quiet afternoons behind billowing curtains, warm salty tasting skin from a sea bath, the promise of a kiss. Finally I smiled.

"I'm Caroline."

"Jason Palmer," he said extending his hand. He held my hand an instant before letting go.

"Sounds familiar."

He cleared his throat. "You know anything about racing?"

"No."

"I used to race Formula 1."

"Maybe that's it."

His mouth curled into a satisfied grin. But his eyes remained hidden behind the mirrored lenses, reflecting sea and the blue and white stripes of parasols. I estimated he was about my age.

"So you're a tourist?"

"God no!" he corrected me. "A visitor. Seeing friends." No one wanted to be identified as a tourist and I'd said it to provoke. Being a tourist meant being an outsider, someone who only stayed for a little while, but didn't really belong. He cringed. The waiter brought his grilled steak with shallots. Jason poked a piece into his mouth. His face darkened a shade and he concentrated on a speed-boat heading toward Cannes. "I needed to get out of the city."

"I know what you mean." I tossed a fringe of long blond hair over my shoulder for effect. It caught his eye. "Most big cities make me feel claustrophobic. That's why I like the sea. There's always a sense of space. You never feel cramped."

"Exactly. What about you?"

"I live here, but I'm from Iowa," I said. "But I don't go back much." He choked or maybe stifled a laugh.

"Iowa. You're about five thousand miles from home."

"Something like that. A small town. I wouldn't go back there to live for anything. Where are you staying?"

"*Hôtel de la Garoupe*." The iron-gated five-star hotel overlooking the bay with the view of the lighthouse popped into mind. It cost at least 450 Euros a night or more. For a moment I felt inferior. Being around people with money had that effect on me, a reaction acquired from my mother who had felt inferior to expensive shop clerks who looked down on her gnarled hands and smirked at her countrified accent. Jason's manicured fingers rubbed up and down the side of the glass; his smooth cheeks and crisp white and blue collar nuzzled against the skin of his neck.

"But you live here?" he said.

"For about five years now."

"Lucky you. I bet lots of people would like to be in you...in your position."

I lifted a fork full of salad to my lips and noticed Jason staring at the diamond studded ring Serge gave me. I wore it because I loved the envious stares and the way the stones flash and glimmer in the sunlight. "We're separated. Getting divorced. But I still think it's beautiful." I wondered if I would have to pawn it to pay the bills or if Serge would come through.

"He takes care of you," Jason said leaning against the canvas back of his chair.

"Did...until he traded me in for a newer model." I laughed and feigned light-heartedness. "We're in court now." I felt like a turtle who wanted to pull its head back into the shell.

"Oh, I'm sorry. Don't clam up. I know how it is. When someone leaves you, you feel full of holes like a target on a shooting range," he said. "But you're beautiful. You'll never be alone." I leaned forward and listened attentively. "You deserve someone better." It seemed like a promise he might fulfill. Another Prince Charming. Jason brushed the back of my hand lightly with his fingertips. The contact sent a shiver up my arm and the hairs stood on end. "You cold?"I shook my head and looked down at my empty plate with the dead anchovies on the edge. He held out a credit card for the waiter. "I'll take care of both," he said motioning to me. Maybe the fairy tale would materialize into something real this time. "Let's go," he said.

A charge of electricity rushed into my heart and it began to pound furiously. I turned away, not wanting to appear eager. But my heart leaped with excitement. In an instant, all of the aches and pains of lost love faded and my emotional canvas was free once again to take on new tints and hues. He was a giant miracle. He touched my hand again and my cheeks flushed with heat.

"Where are we going?" I said. A tiny irritation gnawed at my mind like a small grey mouse. Something inside, something down below. Something felt a bit off, not quite right. But when I searched for reasons not to go, I could find none except for that feeling. It fought with my desire for love and the desire won.

"Come on," he insisted. "I'm going to take you for a ride. You'll love it." He looked perfect: the neatly pressed *Façonnable* shirt; tan jeans; designer sunglasses; a *Rolex* watch. Even the light breeze that blew through his hair tussled it and let it resettle perfectly into place. Julie warned me about handsome men. They're bad news, too self-centered, she'd said. But maybe it was just her rationalization about her plain looking husband, Thomas.

"I need to call Julie and tell her where I am. We're supposed to meet." I excused myself and phoned to tell her that I'd met someone – maybe *the* one, and asked if we could get together a little later than planned.

"Be careful," she warned, always looking out for me. "This isn't Hartsville, Iowa."

"Yes, mom," I joked and we hung up.

I followed Jason up the stairway to the main road, with my *LV* beach bag over my shoulder. He nudged my elbow playfully and guided me toward a silver sports car in the guarded parking lot. It can't be that one, I thought. He dug into his pocket and pulled out the key. The car sat low and curvy near the entrance, the guardian sat right next to it. A Ferrari, I thought, but I acted indifferent. After all, I saw them often on the Riviera. At Juan-les-Pins men drove through the streets slowly with beautiful models beside them to show off. But I'd never been in one and my heart soared. He opened the door for me and I slipped into it casually like it was something I did every day. He slid under the steering wheel. Two couples in the parking lot gawked enviously.

"Let's drive down the A7 to Monaco," he said. The warm smell of new leather tickled my nose and I felt intoxicated by Jason's warmth, all the horse power, the promise of a new romance. He eased the car into first gear and glided onto the seaside road cutting around the Cap d'Antibes. In a few minutes we slipped past the toll booth and cruised down the highway. The speedometer hit 200 km per hour. Trees, mountains and sea raced past in one long blur. I wanted to say, "This is too fast. We're in danger. We need to slow down. Be reasonable." The smallest mistake could send us crashing into a wall or down a cliff. But none of my protests made it out. I shut up and let him drive wildly, like the horses in my dream. The thrill of speed made my cells tingle like when I dived into cold water. I felt suddenly all alive and filled with an adrenaline rush like I hadn't felt so intensely since the last time I fell in love.

***

We met up three days in a row, the first two at the beach restaurant, and on the third day, he invited me to his hotel. We lounged at poolside under a parasol and sipped icy drinks. The smell of warm pines filled the afternoon air, and the planes to and from Nice Airport hummed a continuous, lazy OM. As the heat climbed and the drinks began to take effect, I felt my body throb. It had been so long – too long – and I felt like a bottle of champagne under pressure, about to burst. Jason massaged oil into my back and legs and arms, and the pressure grew. When he bent over to kiss my neck, I sighed deeply and he took me by the hand and led me inside.

"A bottle of champagne for 145," he said into the phone.

"I love to pop the cork," I said. "I used to open the bottles from my terrace and shoot them out to see how far they would fly."

"I bet you won the good-neighbor award," he said. The waiter arrived and set the bottle in a bucket of ice on the table. "Want to try this one?"

"I always say that opening bottles is one reason to have a man around. In fact," I said with a smile. "It may be the only good reason to have one around." Jason unwound the wire cage around the cork and held the bottle at an angle, then skillfully slipped the cork out. It made a slight pop followed by a sigh. "I can think of another good reason." The foamy bubbles dribbled down the edge of a flute glass and he handed me one. "To the three S's."

"Three S's?" I said.

"Sea, sun and..." His voice trailed off.

"No wait, let me guess. Sand?" He laughed, shook his head no. "Synchronicity?"

"No again." He stepped closer.

"Soul. It must be soul."

"After three wrong guesses, you have to pay the consequences." My face turned to the floor, but my eyes looked up. He stood over me now, brushed my hair away from my throat and placed his fingers, cold from the bottle, at the base of my neck. I sipped awkwardly from the glass and spilled half of it down the front of my T. "Oh, what a pity," he said. "Looks like we'll have to do something about that."

"I...I've still got my bikini on underneath."

I felt his breath softly near my cheek and his mouth on my throat. Then the whole world fell away, as if nothing else existed or mattered. The moment expanded into a long, slow flow. In the pink-gold luxury of the evening light as the transparent curtains billowed gently and the cicadas hummed softly, we merged into one.

***

After that Jason often took me to the China Pearl, just behind the city wall near Antibes' port. I liked the aquarium filled with red and gold fish beneath the glass floor. It seemed like we were walking on water. The owner said hello and escorted us to our table by the window. "Your usual," he said.

"Bring us two splits of champagne," Jason said. "We're celebrating."

"Wonderful." I said like a giddy teenager. "You know my weaknesses," I purred. Jason stayed with me sometimes, but traveled often to London. Single girlfriends complained about the lack of suitable men in their thirties, but things were starting to come together for me. He gave direction to my life and helped me make decisions. A waiter brought the bubbly.

"You'll see how well it does. It just keeps rising." He looked at me with soft, liquid eyes and I felt like the most beautiful woman in the world. I'd just given him 70,000 Euros to invest. It was about all that Serge left me with until the settlement.

"Oh, really?" I said suggestively and leaned toward him with my lips pursed. He leaned in close and touched my cheek.

"My London investment banker fiends…friends, are the best," he said. I melted at his warm touch. "They had great returns last year." He promised no risks. His eyes sparkled like little galaxies. Things would be tight, at least until the settlement, I wanted to remind him. But Jason knew the importance of money and I felt I could count on him to help me if Serge didn't come through. He nuzzled my cheek and ran a finger up the pale inside of my forearm, then lifted his glass. I wanted him desperately, wanted to be with him all the time, and I found his absences unbearable. I felt like cords bound us together and we were connected at all of the vital centers – heart, sex, emotion, head. He seeped into my pores until that dark void inside me filled up again. I'd felt so empty and worthless before. But he lifted me up like a powerful ballet dancer lifts his partner and lightly and elegantly spins her around.

"To happy returns," I said lifting my glass for a toast. I felt dizzy with happiness. "I'm so lucky to be with you. That day we hooked up at the beach was no coincidence."

"Destiny?"

"Yes! Everything happens for a reason and we're all where we're supposed to be, meeting the people we're supposed to meet at the right time. Don't you think?" He shrugged.

"That's a big thought," he said

We finished the curries with ginger and lemon grass and ended the meal with rose-scented, rice liqueur in thimble-sized glasses, an offering from the owner on the house. I stared into the transparent liquid and focused on the ceramic glass with a lens at the bottom. A muscle-bound, tanned man stared back at me, his muscles flexed. They used to give glasses with whistles on the side to women and the glasses with lenses at the bottom to men. I turned up the contents and swallowed the sharp tasting alcohol and when I looked into it again, the man had disappeared. One moment there and the next moment he was gone. "There was a naked man in the bottom of my glass."

"Fortunately, I got a woman in mine. Kind of cute, but not pretty like you."

***

I dress up all in white today – an Indian style blouse and tight white jeans for the drive down the *Corniche* to Monaco. English-bred Julie lives there in her tax-free luxury. We agreed to meet at the *Thermes*, the seawater baths perched on a rock cliff above the Principality's harbor, for a few hours of self-indulgence. We exercise in the glassed-in workout room, before slipping into the mud wraps and saunas, and then lounge leisurely by the mosaic-tiled pool filled with seawater. Stretched out on the lounge chair, I think of Jason in London as I watch the yachts bob in the distance. A gentle cascade of water flows into the pool. I nestle down into my thick, cotton bathrobe and enter that dreamy space mid-way between waking consciousness and sleep. In an instant the horse rumbles past my vision again. The same one from the dream. Its hooves pound hard against the earth and shake me back to tense alertness.

"I hate that," I say out loud.

"You really jumped," Julie sits up and her elbow sinks into the thick mattress.

"Horses," I whisper.

"What?"

"Oh, nothing. Just..." I concentrate vaguely on the white-hulled yachts in the harbor below. "What do horse dreams mean?"

Julie sits up, fully attentive now. She loves these kinds of questions. She remains silent for a few seconds, her preternaturally green eyes look upward toward the domed ceiling.

"You still there? Or did you just go off into *samadhi*?" I say sarcastically.

"Jung would say it's all related to your associations. It's probably about your animal nature."

"And Freud would say it's all about sex."

"Oh, he's wrong. We're really more highly evolved than that."

"Speak for yourself," I say joking, but she doesn't laugh.

"Can you tell me more?"

"Yes, doctor," I say facetiously and tell her about the dream. "It probably doesn't mean anything."

"Did you ride?"

"Yes, and I owned one once. But I was just a kid then."

"Hum," Julie says. "How's Jason?"

"God, he's so wonderful, like a dream come true. Not a nightmare like Serge. He's in London. I miss him." Julie raises a limp hand to draw the attention of a waiter.

"*De l'eau, s'il vous plait,*" she says. He returns with a chilled glass bottle of *Evian* and two glasses. "They're symbols," Julie says.

"Huh?"

"The horses. We can't take the truth head on, so the soul feeds us symbols," she says. "It uses the indirect approach."

I get irritated at the mention of the S word. A soul. "It was probably just caused by something I ate."

"Could be," Julie says. "But then again maybe not. How do the dreams make you feel?"

"Scared, like I'm going to fall and get hurt."

"Consider it," Julies says. "Horses can be wild and destructive unless they're tamed. Think of the expressions, 'horsing around', 'horse power', 'dark horse'." I sit up on one elbow.

"Really? All of that from a horse?"

"By the way, when are you going to introduce us? Thomas and I would like to meet him."

"Sure, fine," I say, but for some unidentifiable reason, I feel uncomfortable about it.

"Thomas gets back from South Africa on Friday. Let's do it over the weekend."

"Okay," I reluctantly agree.

***

Jason just returned from London and we're supposed to meet at the port. I see Jason's car. A tourist wearing a flower print shirt hovers over it with a girl in a bikini leaning into him.

"That's too cool."

"Yeah," the guy says. "I like the logo."

I walk past them and see Jason talking to a woman by the round port office. When he sees me coming, he tenses; she smiles slyly in my direction, then slips behind him and walks onto an expensive wooden-hulled yacht and disappears below deck.

"Hey beautiful," he says and wraps his arms around me. "I missed you."

"Who was that?"

"Oh, she was asking for directions."

"Oh." He kisses me and then I latch onto his hand. "Why did you stay away so long?" It's an accusation rather than a question.

"I had some meetings."

"What kind?" I moan jealously.

"You should just be happy I'm back," he says.

We amble along the quay past the yachts with teak decks and brass fittings, past white motorboats. They bear names like My Last Dream, Greatest Ambition, On The Edge, Moonbeam. Most of the boats sit in the port all year long as a tribute to the realized aspirations of harried businessmen who earn success, then have no time to enjoy it.

"Let's go to the China Pearl again," I say lightly. His face darkens with the dusk and he turns inward and quiet. I trail behind him. Notice his walk. It's crooked. I want to feel light-hearted and even skip along the quay toward the old town. But an anchor like a lead weight pulls me down. A few feet away where the fishermen's boats dock, a huge fish hangs upside down with its jaws open. A shark. I do not celebrate its being drawn to the surface. Sometimes a rare one gets caught in the nets and dragged ashore. It lives in the darkness of the depths and looks fierce with its gapping jaws and always hungry. It's just their nature.

"I snagged one once on a fishing trip," Jason brags.

"That size?"

"Bigger."

"You must have been fishing pretty deep," I say. "It's a pilgrim shark. They rarely ever surface."

"Of course, I know that," he says.

"Let's go eat," I say. A gray sensation bordering on discomfort starts to rise up inside me like a dense fog. I let go of his hand as we walk toward the restaurant, and I think of money.

***

Horses again. One knocks me on the ground. I jerk up from a dream and stop it before the hard fall. It's the same dream. Another woman is on a horse too. She stops me. Grabs my arm, whispers a secret in my ear, a secret I do not want to hear. She points to the hanging shark. I shake my head. Reach out to find Jason's warm body snuggled beneath the sheets, but he's not there. My mind races, my heart pounds. Something underneath. Something…then I fall into a light sleep again to escape and forget.

***

Julie invites us to the Monte-Carlo Country Club for a tennis match. "They've heard your name and think maybe you've met at a party. They're from London too." Jason clenches his fists, his jaws are tight. We argued during the morning. Jason didn't want to go and I almost cancelled. "You'll love the place – and them."

"I've already been," he says. "I hate the clay courts. They turn my socks red."

"Who did you go with?" It takes two to play, I think.

"A school mate invited me. A good chap with a bad backhand. He was easy to defeat."

I'm relieved it wasn't a woman. Sometimes he makes me feel so insecure the way his eyes wander. I feel he's always looking for other possibilities, never quite satisfied. Julie and Thomas meet us on the court. Julie wears a pale blue dress and Thomas is all in white, just like Jason. Thomas thrusts his thick hand at Jason before grabbing me and kissing me on each cheek. "How's the lady?" he booms. Tall and burly, Thomas towers over us all. Jason steps back.

Thomas studies him. "So you were a racecar driver?"

"Yes. You're from London too?" Jason stiffens, glances around the court. Thomas fixes him in a gaze. Jason bounces a ball on the court impatiently with his tennis racket.

"Yes, but we prefer it here. I feel certain that we've met somewhere," Julie says with a smile, but her eyes scrutinize him.

"Shall we start?" Jason says.

"We already wet down the court." Thomas adds.

We volley back and forth to warm up. Thomas and Julie on one side and I'm with Jason on the other. Playing doubles, they're already in sync, finely tuned to each other's weaknesses. Thomas covers for Julie's weak backhand. Julie covers for Thomas's lack of speed in getting to the net. Jason and I just begin to feel out each other's moves. After the first set, we take a break, swig bottled water and Gatorade. Jason and I are behind.

"I'm not used to the sun," he complains.

Thomas smirks. He lumbers over me and stands with his racket poised on his shoulder. "So where did you grow up, Mr. Palmer?" It's not a friendly question.

"We moved around a lot," Jason sips from a bottle. His smile resembles a snarl, then softens when he catches me studying him quizzically.

"Do you know Lady Halsey? I think we may have met at one of her dinners in London," Thomas says.

"She certainly has her boy-toys. It's a wonder Lord Halsey doesn't make a scene," Julie blurts, then bites her lip as if she said too much.

Jason shrugs.

"What schools did you go to?" Thomas says.

Jason turns away and walks onto the court. Julie must have told Thomas that Jason drives a Ferrari. But Thomas is not easily impressed by clothes or cars or any sort of status symbols. He wants to know Jason's history, examine his character. I feel Thomas's paternalism. He wants to protect me.

"Enough of the inquisition," I say.

"Just trying to get to know the chap," Thomas says. Jason strolls back to join us.

Julie hands Thomas a can of new balls to open. "This is your job," she says. "I always say that there are only a few good reasons to have a man around. And opening cans is one of them."

"Caroline says the same thing." Jason bounces a ball and the nervous rhythm irritates me.

"Spending their money is another," Thomas says.

We walk back onto the court and Julie and Thomas consistently beat us set by set until we reach the end. "I guess Jason and I need to get to know each other better," I say to Julie.

"Oh, we have a ten year advantage. At this point, we read each other's minds," she says. We shower and then meet up for a drink by the pool. The Mediterranean stretches out below us, wide and virtually borderless. Julie and I arrive first.

"And they say women take a long time!"

"Oh they must be preening," Julie says.

Julie orders a bottle of *prosecco* to celebrate their victory and my new relationship. Thomas and Jason shuffle to the table and she pours the sparkling wine and lifts a glass. "To true love."

"You know what they say?" Thomas says. "Love is blind."

"Desire is blind," Julie says. "Not love."

"Since when are they different?" I wonder out loud. Julie rolls her eyes as if I'm clueless.

"You're too philosophical for me," Jason says. Thomas swigs from his glass while Jason studies his manicured nails. Julie removes the sparkling wine from the ice bucket and refills our glasses.

"Jason says he knows some good London investment bankers," I chirp. "He's advised me on where to put some money. Maybe you know them too, Thomas."

"Oh, do tell," Thomas insists.

"Let's talk about something more exciting," Jason says.

"Money's always an exciting subject," Thomas quips.

"These are private matters," Jason says.

"I'm okay talking about it. They're my best friends," I say. But his lips clamp shut.

"How long have you known each other?" Thomas says.

"About six weeks, I suppose. Close to two months, really." I look to Jason for support. "I know it seems fast."

"But there was a feeling between us from the very beginning," he says.

"It's truly special," I add.

Thomas grimaces like he might gag, then his phone rings. I breathe a sigh of relief as he excuses himself to answer.

"I'm sorry about him," Julie says. "He's a little out of sorts for some reason. It's work pressure, I guess."

***

Julie calls the next morning. "Let's have lunch today," she says cheerily. "I'll come to Antibes." I know it's something serious because she rarely wants to drive the 45 minutes through tourist traffic.

"Okay."

"Can we do it *tête á tête*?"

I look over at Jason who's still unshaven. I form the word "Julie" in a whisper with my lips. He frowns back at me. "Sure, is something wrong?" I tell her.

"Oh no, of course not. I'd just like to see you."

"Great! Where should we go?"

"How about the Garoupe? I like the *Keller Plage*."

"Fine, see you later."

"You guys getting together today?"

"Yeah, I guess she wants to talk." Jason gets up and showers. In a few minutes, the spicy scent of shaving cream and aftershave fill the hallway. He emerges wearing a white towel wrapped around his waist. "I'm heading back to London today."

"When did you decide that?"

"I just realized there's something I need to take care of."

"Shall I take you to the airport?"

"No. I'll drive. Incidentally, your investment is doing very well. You might consider transferring more money. Don't want to miss out on an opportunity like that."

"When will they send a statement?"

"In a few weeks. You should get something every quarter," he says. He stuffs his leather toiletries case into a carry-on bag along with his toothbrush, aftershave, and the underwear and t-shirts he'd left in a drawer. "You're taking all of your things? You know you can leave them."

"I know, but I'll need these."

"You'll be away for a few days then."

"I don't know. A couple of days at least." He looks handsome, irresistible in his tight white polo shirt and light blue denims. I want to beg him not to go.

"Whatever," I say and kiss him on the neck. I miss him already.

"I'll call," he says and slips out the door. I run out after him and watch the car pull away.

***

Julie and I chit chat, but I know there's something she's waiting to say. After we finish our salads and settle down into the padded chairs, she clears her throat.

"How well do you know Jason?" I shrug.

"How well do I know myself? How well does anyone know anyone? Why?"

"Thomas is concerned." I clench my water glass and sit up straight. "Have you ever met any of his friends or family?"

"No."

"Thomas didn't have a good feel about him."

"I thought you'd met before."

"Well that's just it."

"Is this a silly intuition thing?" My eyes narrow. My mouth grows taut and stern and I look out to the sea to shift my mind away from her face. Julie looks apologetic. "You always say that whatever we see is a reflection of ourselves. Right?"

She nods.

"You see a thief, then you're a thief inside. You see a saint, then you're a saint too."

"Yes, I did say that. But it's not always so simple."

She seems surprised that I remembered so well. "Thomas must see something about himself."

"You know he's well connected. Of course, he's checking it out with some of our mutual friends, but…"

"No. Don't. Do me a favor and stay out of our business."

"But it's for you."

"Stop."

"Jason's a…"

I scoot my chair back, stand up and toss the napkin on the table. "I need support now, not lectures. Excuse me." My eyes burn and I walk to the restroom to wash my face in cold water.

***

A few days later, when the sun reaches its zenith, I descend the steps of my villa. I'll have to move out soon; it'll be sold as part of the settlement. The click, click of my high heeled sandals against the stone steps mingles with the rhythmic hum of the cicadas. I slide into the car, and pull on sunglasses and a white, visor to protect me from the harsh noonday sun. The car engine idles quietly and I edge it out of the shade of the garage and onto the road. At this hour, the town is lethargic, functioning at the rhythm of knives and forks clinking against porcelain plates from lunches on outdoor terraces. Cicadas hum and stretch out the afternoon while a light sea breeze stirs the palm leaves. I look forward to seeing Jason's smiling face at the airport soon.

I wind past the fountain on the port, past the roundabout toward the stone wall of the ramparts. The sea fills the horizon edged by the Cap with the lighthouse perched on the hill in the distance. The water shimmers and glints. In the rearview mirror I notice a woman with thick blonde hair and a black headband driving a black Mercedes very close behind. Did she follow me to Monaco earlier? I head towards the Cap and turn off of the main road toward the lighthouse and then down a narrow side street where few tourists

go. The woman in the car follows. Her determined face hidden behind black-lensed glasses haunts me. I turn the wrong way down
a short one-way street before reconnecting with the main road that
winds around the Cap again. The woman no longer trails me, but
my mind worries and wonders and whispers possible scenarios of
who she might be and what she wants.

***

Jason calls to ask about me. "Did you take care of it like you said
you would?"

"Take care of what?"

"The transfer." I feel suddenly very flat, like a lead weight just
fell on me; my legs move heavily until I sit down in the over-stuffed
chair in the living room.

"I had lunch with Julie. Besides it's not like I've got much left,
you know."

"They don't like me."

"Where are you?"

"London. You're investment's doing well. I saw the bankers today. I wouldn't put it off too long. They're expecting a big jump in
returns this year."

"It's a good connection. Sounds like you're next door. Why
don't I come to meet you? You can introduce me to your friends
and family. I can meet the bankers too."

"Sure, but not this time. Wait a few weeks."

"A few weeks!" Disappointment weighs me down. "When are
you coming home?"

"I'm anxious to get back there. Did Thomas say anything?"
Jason says.

"No."

"He didn't like me."

"What's with you two?"

"You can't please everyone. *C'est la vie.*"

"I miss you. I'd really like to come over just for a day or two. We could go to a show."

"Not now," he insists. "Listen I've got to go. Going through a tunnel. See you soon."

"I love you," I say.

"Me too," he says. You love you too? I think, and the line goes dead.

***

I unlatch the gate to go for an evening walk under the tall pines. The blonde middle-aged woman who I'd seen following me, waits in her black Mercedes across the street. She smokes a cigarette. I courageously walk up to her window and wave hello to let her know I've noticed her. She stubs out the cigarette in the ashtray, then fingers a button and her window glides down. Her narrow sharp face and pointy nose give her an eagle-like quality.

"Are you looking for something?" I say a bit haugtily.

"My car. Where's my car?" she growls like an angry dog. I make a joke of it, step back, eye the Mercedes.

"Looks like you're sitting in it."

"Where's the Ferrari? I know he's been with you, so where's he left it? Her inch long pink fingernails click against the steering wheel and her eyes bore into me.

"Your car?" I say confused.

"He went around telling everyone he was a racecar driver. Such a lot of rot. He's a two bit gigolo. He's probably gone back to London." Her sharp-tongued words hit their mark and my lips twist up like I just tasted something bitter. She smirks. "You're just one of many, honey. But I hope you were wiser than me. That car's worth over 300 grand. My husband will kill me if he finds out." She hands me her card. "If you see Jason again, call me. Please." Her tone is more conciliatory now, sentimental and pleading. "He was good fun. Too bad he turned out to be such a prick." She revs her motor and puts the car in first gear.

I study her card – Pamela Duprès – with an address in Cap Ferrat, one in London, and another in the Caymans. She blows her nose and screeches out of the parking space, stops to evaluate me. "You're not bad." She looks haggard. "Bastard," I hear her say just before she drives out of earshot. She throws a photo out of the car window. It settles at my feet. It's Jason standing by the Ferrari with his arms around her and he's smiling seductively. My eyes zero in on the logo. It's the silver horse reared back on its hind legs like in my dreams. Its mane blows in the wind and the dreams make some sense. Warnings to pay attention, to watch out.

A wave of hurt mixed with nausea kicks up from my gut. I feel sick and disgusted with myself, like I ate something that was too sweet even when I knew it was bad for me. And all the time another part of me, that wiser part, was trying to show me the truth that I didn't want to see – that I didn't need him, that he was bad for me. I run down to the sea, my sandals clicking against the pavement. I strip and plunge off of a rock into the depths. When I surface the tears come, but no one knows you're crying if you're in the sea. The salty tears mingle with the salty sea and wash away the pain. And the dreams…if only I'd listened to the dreams and the wise one inside of me who knew. Now I know.

Chapter 11
Appeasing Kali

"I'm not sure where I am," Caroline says to a middle-aged man with dark skin and a serene face.

"Well, where did you come from?" His Indian accent sounds pleasant, soft to her ears. It lilts with the ends of the words rising up as if perpetually asking a question. She had stopped in front of the women sitting on the ground stringing together garlands of orange and white flowers. Woven baskets lodged between their legs, and their fingers worked nimbly one by one linking each flower to the next to form long chains. The jasmine will wilt in the day's heat, she had thought as they called out to her in high pitched voices, "Buy some ma'am? Flowers for Kali." The silent air shimmered. An ox trudged by pulling a cart filled with milk canisters. And then she quietly slipped into a space – the witness, present, empty of thought, yet completely full and aware, a space that stretched out timeless and eternal. When the secret, sacred moment had passed she found herself back on the street with everything transformed. Dirt roads shot off in five directions and none of them looked familiar.

She squints, examines the places. One stall after another sells postcards, idols, incense. "I came from that direction I think." She points at the second street and begins to walk toward it, one doubt-filled step at a time. Thigh-high kids with short black hair and eyes as dark and soft as a velvety summer's night touch the white skin of her elbow and reach for her hand. The man speaks to them in a language she does not know and they move away.

"They rarely see blonde hair like yours," the man says apologizing. Caroline tries to smile at him, but feels lost, worried. *How will I get back? Where am I?* Four days ago they had left Antibes – comfortable, familiar, home – to end up here. The flight attendant announced their arrival in Mumbai, but the place feels so foreign that Caroline wonders if the plane had not bounced out of the atmosphere and missed the earth altogether and landed on another planet a billion miles away. If Julie were here, she would know the way. But she lies in bed at the hotel with fever and dysentery. Maybe she will shift her love for India to a place that knows how to respond to her affections in a less violent way.

As she observes the streets, the country assaults her senses – odors of saffron, turmeric and curry; the caress of the wind carries sandalwood and amber; the heat bears down on her head; the monkeys screech and the over-sized crows caw. Even the butterflies, the size of her two hands joined together, seem possessed by some vibrant, pulsating energy. At dawn, the prayer tower cut through her sleepy sea of consciousness with a loud call to bow to Allah. Hindu priests promenaded through the streets chanting and clapping, encircling the shrines of their gods at five-thirty a.m. A line of darkly skeletal women rose and waited at the temple gates to get a place inside – she saw them gathering silently like ghosts when she had stirred and looked out the window. Later their voices rose together under the high gilded roof and expanded into the cosmos where they say all things coalesce, lose form and merge. Julie said in a sleepy voice that their song was a morning prayer to awaken God lest he might oversleep and the whole world would cease to function. Could the world vanish in an instant?

Caroline squints at the bright light and covers her head with a scarf for shelter from the sun. A slew of intensely colored, three-wheeled rickshaw taxis with idols and sacred cows glued to dash boards buzz around honking, throwing up trails of dust and puffs of black smoke. She covers her mouth and dodges them to cross the street. A driver stops, leans out the side. "I give you a ride. You go with me?"

No. She shakes her head and walks on. Ninety-six degrees yesterday, she thinks, and they said it could get hotter. Julie said that even the shop owners who can afford it move to cooler climes – and they'll be leaving soon too, when Julie's intestines make peace with the parasites. If only she were back home. She thinks of the Mediterranean Sea, its soulful blue, the cool breeze and its constant presence like a loyal companion. Her adoration of it, her yearning to be enveloped by it, is the closest she has ever come to devotion and yearning for a god. She wants to go back to her comfortable queen bed, to long hot showers and French restaurants with chilled rosé.

"What is the name of your hotel?" The soft-spoken man walks at her elbow, his eyes filled with concern, remind her she is lost in India.

She stops, turns, aware of him again. "Oh…uh, Santi something, I think. But it was just right here. I couldn't have gone far." She looks anxiously at the roads. Her eyes fill up like a blue glacier lake at the foot of the Himalayas about to overflow.

"Have you had nothing to eat?"

The smell of deep-fried sweets tickles her nose; her tummy growls loudly. The lake of her tears spills onto the street.

"My wife is right here." His thin finger points behind them to a small woman bartering for garlands of flowers. He waves at her. The woman's eyes move from Caroline to the man and back. She carries orange garlands of delicate flowers that flow down her arms and the pleats of her yellow sari billow out as she walks. Caroline wipes her eyes. The man speaks to his wife and she shakes her head from side to side as if someone holds her chin to pull it from left to right. Caroline does not know if it means yes or no; the woman does not look into her eyes. "Come and we will offer you some sweet chai and *gulab jamun*. It will give you time to calm down and when your mind is at rest, you will remember."

"No, really," Caroline says. "I'll find it." And she wants to go on alone, but when she looks into the streets, she feels small and helpless like a lone child lost in an immense department store. The things that filled her eyes with delight and drew her away from safety lose all appeal. A sense of panic begins to rise from her stomach to her throat and she's afraid of crying out. She turns to him as a last resort. "Are you sure it's okay?" Her eyes plead. He smiles and the woman walks ahead of them, a long trail of silk covers her shoulder, but reveals the flesh of her back at the midriff. They enter a street with ancient trees and open front houses with intricate chalk designs at the doorways. Old women squat out front or sit on crates. They pass a young woman ironing clothes with an iron heated over burning coal. Caroline peers into the darkness of the houses, but nothing is revealed. God's face smiles out from shrines along the way. A blue-skinned Shiva sits cross legged, one hand held up in a blessing. A river flows through his hair and a necklace of serpents hangs around his neck. If he knew the way, it looks like his lips would never open to reveal it.

The wife stops at a threshold and kicks off her leather sandals on a mat. The woman and her husband look so much alike they could be twins. The man follows. "Please," he says. His face looks fatherly and his soft words mesmerize Caroline into following.

"Please," he repeats and motions for her to step in front of him. She removes her silver sandals and goes inside. A Hindi film of Kashmir mountains blinks sporadically on the eye of the old TV. Songs accompanied by the drone of reed flutes and a sitar ripple through the incense perfumed rectangle of a room. The woman calls out and a hunched, toothless grandmother arrives sliding her feet over the floor with a child groping at her skirt.

No introductions are made. Names seem unnecessary here, like matter that drives a wedge between the essence of a thing and its appearance. In the space where words and names dissolve, truth becomes visible. The wife sets about hanging flowers over the neck of a goddess that adorns the center of the room. Caroline's distress at being lost grows in the presence of the black-faced statue; in one hand the goddess holds a sword, in another of her many hands she holds a grotesque head. Caroline observes the wife from the corner of her eye. Her hands are held together in submission. The grandmother lights incense and mutters something punctuated with drool and a blissful smile.

When the women finish, the man wearing white cotton pants covered with a long tunic, faces her. "Will you have hot tea?" Caroline nods. His wife pats a pillow at the goddess's feet, motioning for Caroline to sit. Choked with incense and despair, tears fill her eyes. Her heart pounds with anxiety. The mindless hum of the old woman plucks at her nerves. The wife disappears and then returns with two metal cups and hands one to Caroline and the other to her husband. It burns Caroline's fingers and she quickly sets it on the floor and stares into the murky water. Will some minute invisible life form in there reduce her to a ball of writhing flesh, like it did Julie? The man sits on a cushion beside her and extends a plate of deep-fried dough shaped into balls. "You like Indian sweets?"

She politely accepts one, wraps it discreetly in a tissue she takes from her pocket, and wipes the sticky syrup from her fingers. She slides the sweet in her purse when the man looks away. The wife disappears into the black shadow of an anteroom. Caroline holds the metal cup between her hands, rolling it nervously back and forth. Her breathing rises and falls nervously. "My friend's sick at the hotel. I thought I could find my way around alone."

"We will get you home," he says. "But try to enjoy the moment."

"In case I die in the next few minutes?" She looks up warily at the goddess and wonders about human sacrifice.

"You could, but chances are you won't. It's good to live like you might though. It makes you appreciate life more." Her eyes narrow at him in distrust. His voice flows out unhurried and soothing. "I believe in your part of the world you say, 'Carpe Diem.' Seize the day."

She takes a deep breath and sighs. "Everything's strange here." India reminds her of the first time she went diving. On the surface, the instructor made the okay sign to her and she smiled through the mask and signed back okay. She truly felt it would be okay, but when he held onto her harness and pulled her into the blue, she automatically jerked her head up for air. It's not my environment. I can't breath, she wanted to scream. But they were already on their way down and she saw nothing but blue for a long time until the red cliffs of the underwater mountains came into view ten meters below.

He listens, sips his tea. "You like it?"

She sips warily, then puckers her lips. "I hope it doesn't kill me."

The man chuckles. "Time will kill you. Tea won't." She tenses her brow and shakes her head. "What is your name?"

"Caroline."

"Does it mean anything?"

"I don't know. I don't think so. It's just a name. Does yours?"

"I am Krishna."

She looks back into a memory of American men with shaved heads dressed in orange robes chanting the name at an airport. "Hari Krishna."

"Lord Krishna. He was a god and Radha was his greatest devotee and lover."

"Oh." Caroline sips the tea tasting of cardamom and stares vacantly off into the past back to Serge walking away, then Jason. She wonders if she'll see them again. "Do you believe in reincarnation?" she says.

Krishna lifts his tea to his dark lips, blows on the surface of the liquid, then he drinks. "It's certainly plausible."

"We will see our ex-husbands and lovers again?" Her heart fills with hope and dread. If only she could do it all over again, she would be better, wiser. She stares into the flame of a lamp burning on the altar. Desperation had driven her to this. It had started long before, the pang of emptiness, the haunting loneliness even in a crowd, even with Serge or Jason beside her. Despair had so filled her one night that she grasped for reasons not to quit. The window sill was easy to reach. She slid the chair beside it, unlatched the window that blew back with a burst of wind. Her foot found a sturdy place on the seat, her knee flexed, and her body rose up so that the sill was only half a step away. Looking down into the night from so high up, she saw the void below, the void which represented her own hollow self.

In that moment she remembered her rich things: the Persian rugs, the silver, crystal, and bone china. They were like props in a play that had no meaning. Her right foot lifted to join the left one on the chair automatically. Her lungs stretched to fill with sea air as she stared out into the darkness where she knew the sea waited in silence. She had nothing more to do but lean out, chest forward and fly out the window. But as she looked up a fire in the sky shimmered, reflected back the tiny spark of life that remained and was about to be extinguished in the pointless stupidity of her daily existence. Then a decision, like a miracle arrived. There had to be something more and she would find it.

Krishna's wide dark eyes look vast and full, like staring into that night sky. Embarrassment flushes her cheeks. Can he see into her heart and read the headlines of her past like a tabloid newspaper? "I guess we'd have to go through puberty again too. Pimples and all."

He seems to accept her and not judge. "It's God sporting."

She scratches her head, reflects. "Oh you mean he has a sense of humor and the jokes on us." He blows on the tea making ripples in the surface and tilts the cup to his lips. "What happens if you don't want to play the game anymore?"

"I think it's like a merry-go-round. When you get tired of it you can get off."

"And then what?"

"You go Home."

The mention of home sends a dart of pain through her heart. She sits up on her knees and looks into the face of the goddess towering three feet high over Caroline now, hideous and hellish. "I need to go."

"You are a good person. You will find your way."

No, I'm not good she wants to say, not if you really knew me. "The hotel is called Pa..santi or Par Shanthi."

"You know what Shanthi is?"

The goddess stares wildly at her. What is that garland carved in stone around her neck?

"Peace. Peace that knows no bounds."

"Oh," she says. As she pronounces the word it seems to transform into OM against her will.

"Let's go. We will find it. I will ask someone down the street."

"Why are you helping me?" She eyes him suspiciously, but his warm eyes laugh back at her suspicion and a smile breaks across his face like dawn after a dark night.

"We are taught to treat all people as our guests, because all are embodiments of God."

She blinks, closes her eyes against him, then stares back. The thought that she could be God makes her want to alternately laugh and cry. Does God get lost too?

**

Out in the heat, the sun rises toward noon and they walk down a tree-lined lane. "Have you been to the U.S.?"

"Yes, I went there to study. But I came back for my mother."

Another old woman, withered, and ancient, sets nine small clay pots on an altar built at the base of a tree and sticks a wick in each one, then fills them with oil from a jug. Caroline stops, focuses until all else falls away. The still air hums with mantras from the priest in the nearby temple. "Ram, Ram, Aaauuummm." People shuffle past in a flow of color – lime green, royal blues, gold, silver, orange, red and whites, especially whites.

"Do you know Ganesha?" Krishna points to the elephant-faced god with a paunch smiling contentedly. A priest stands behind the shrine gate breaking coconuts.

"No."

"He removes obstacles."

Devotees walk round and round Ganesha, while the monkeys steal the offerings of cucumbers and bananas and prance around on the shrine railing with their butts in the air.

"What's she doing?" She points to the ancient woman circling the tree clockwise carrying a lit oil lamp and chanting softly.

Caroline concentrates on the unwavering light and stands trans-
fixed. The air glistens like in a mirage and the old woman dressed
in a gold trimmed white sari lights the remaining lamps one by
one. Slowly. Carefully. Dutifully. Fully concentrated on the task.
In the rhythm and the flow, it seems this ritual – lighting the lamp,
of offering worship to some god, of reaching out to the essence
that makes us grow, and glow and sustains us until we die and
become suffused with the element of eternity – has continued un-
ceasing for eons on end. Caroline stands there engulfed in silence,
her mind empty, her heart beginning to fill. The ancient woman
finishes her turning and chanting, then offers Caroline some of the
food meant for the god. At first she refuses, embarrassed. But the
woman delivers a toothy smile and insists.

"A sweet *ladoo*," Krishna says behind her. "Prasad. Don't worry. It's blessed food to feed God. It won't make you sick." Julie said
she once drank water from the Ganges that had been blessed by a
priest. Though it contained sewage and cadavers she didn't fall ill.
So Caroline warily accepts and nibbles a piece of the sweet. The
dark gnarled hand of a stooped man appears at Caroline's elbow
and the poor woman gladly fills it too.

"Does absolutely everything here mean something more than it
seems?" she says, annoyed.

Last night the divinities invaded her dreams. They'd been
seeping in from the time she first arrived, cavorting and cajoling,
fasting and threatening. A nine foot tall monkey plunged its hands
into a lake and withdrew a big fish.The fish would certainly not
get away. The monkey mind, the title of a book she saw in a store
window, taming the monkey mind. India's gods were merging into
her, permeating the depths of her being like the subtle sounds of
the reed flute weaving through the air. She awakens from her rev-
erie to the high pitched notes and follows the music a short distance to the source – a man wearing a turban. A cobra's eyes peek

out of a rotund basket; its body rises and sways. The man's breath rushes through the flute, holding the unpredictable creature suspended under his invisible control. She looks for a thread or a trick and crosses to the other side of the street, bemused, but distrustful of the power of music over the poisonous nature of the animal.

"It's just the music, right?"

Krishna smiles, but offers no explanation.

She studies the one room wooden shops, the dusty streets and hand-painted signs and throws her hands up in an exasperated sign of surrender. "This isn't the way! It all looks the same."

Shopkeepers try to wave her inside. "Come see my Kanchi silks." "Perfumed oils from Madras, lady." "You like gold jewellery and rubies?" Her pace quickens, until Krishna stops.

"I'll ask here," he says pointing to a small group of men. She waits and unconsciously reaches out to finger the fabrics hanging in the doorway and hears Krishna pronounce the word "Shanthi." Crossing the threshold, she follows the beautiful silks, touching one and then another until she forgets she is lost.

"Welcome," he says. "What would you like? Some hot tea? A cold drink?"

"No, thanks."

"You are our guest." He wears a serious smile. "Please have something to drink. At least take some bottled water."

Caroline relents. "Some water would be nice."

The man sports a pair of black jeans and a polo shirt and calls to someone behind an opaque paisley curtain. A boy runs out and disappears down the street.

"The fan feels nice in this heat." The store is like a wooden box with no windows. Inside unfinished wooden shelves line the walls to the ceiling. A bright silk image of Buddha with his heart radiating rays of energy hangs on the central wall at the back. The scented oils soothe her anxiety as she lifts the testers to her nose one by one – lotus, jasmine, rose. She admires silks brocaded with thick bands of gold, pashmina shawls, and hand-embroidered pillows from Kashmir. By the time she makes her way around the stall about the size of a small hotel room, the boy returns with a chilled bottle of water. The man takes it from him and hands it to Caroline.

"It's sealed," he reassures her. Caroline twists off the lid and drinks. Her eyes fall on a delicate white lotus. "It comes from the Himalayas. A stone carver does them for me. Here is a Buddha too." He points to a jade head with eyes half-open, a look of impenetrable serenity on its face.

"It's very beautiful. But who could ever be so calm?"

"Think of it as something to aspire to."

Her eyes trace back to the black statues of the dancer encircled with flames and the woman wearing a garland. It is the same goddess that haunted Krishna's house. "Are those heads?"

"That's Kali."

"Not very friendly."

"And Shiva, the destroyer."

"Why love a god who destroys?"

"They worship all aspects of life."

"You're not Hindu?" she said.

"I am Buddhist. We worship no thing." Tonkas of bodhisattvas lost in meditation under bodhi trees hang in a back corner.

"May I see it?"

"Kali?" She nods. He reaches up and plucks the statue from the shelf. "Here."

"Does it make sense to you?" She examines the image.

"I think she teaches humility."

Kali, the name forms silently on her lips. The goddess cuts

through her mental garble straight to the quick of her psyche. Where other gods wear flowers or jewels, she sports a garland of human heads. Others seek to console and offer compassion, but Kali makes no such pretence. Life is hard. Birth hurts. Death does too. All things that she has created she will also destroy. Nothing lasts forever and she makes no apologies.

"Shiva's consort. A goddess of love."

"Of love?" Caroline imagines her dancing on human hearts and laughing at her misery.

"I think I've found the hotel," Krishna says appearing next to her and he points at the statue. "You like her?"

She briefly looks up to acknowledge him.

"Ramakrishna saw Kali walk out of the Ganges like a pregnant princess, give birth to her child on the river bank, then turn into a monster with dreadful jaws and consume it," the shopkeeper says and hands her some postcards: a black statue dressed in gold jewels and a red silk sari, tongue hanging out as if in lust, the face of a wild woman. Caroline hears a voice in her heart: terrible, beautiful, painful, blissful. *Kali merges all into her Self beyond contradiction, beyond comprehension. As she is, so is life. She rises up then fades away just as quickly and quietly as she appeared. No one however strong or wealthy and powerful nor meek and good and innocent or evil escapes her grip. No different is she than the mystery of Time, itself.*

"She treats all the same," Krishna says.

Caroline remembers Jason, how hope and promise of replacing Serge metamorphosed into remorse and regret. It's easy to see in retrospect, to analyze the mistakes and understand the motives that were hidden, even from herself. Being empty, she wanted someone to fill her up and make her whole, someone who would take care of her. In Jason, she found someone who was looking for the same thing. Needy human beings, like black holes, suck everything into them indiscriminately. If she had not been so self-absorbed, then

she would have listened to her heart and seen through his deception. Instead, in her desire-filled blindness, she had only deceived
herself. This is what hurt most. She had abandoned her Self. That
was her sin.

"You don't have sinners." Caroline looks from Krishna to the
clerk. "Either of you?" Then her thoughts continue without waiting for a response as if Kali, staring back at her, forms the answers
directly in her heart. *Where would joy be without sadness, or love
without hatred? Both determine the value of the other and each owes its
existence to its opposite.* Caroline temporarily shifts her eyes to the
jade Buddha, its head the size of hers. *Isn't this the mystery of life
unveiled,* he seems to say – *to accept all as essential and necessary with
equanimity?* There is some comfort in this – when failure and success, life and death all seem vital and yet totally irrelevant in the
scheme of things.

But Kali is the goddess to appease and fear. *If you are a destroyer,
then I offer you my garland of fear and pain and emptiness,* she thinks
and mentally lays it at Kali's feet. Kali accepts. In her mind's eye,
a steady flame like the one from the old woman's lamp, rises and
burns her offering into a raging fire. Caroline's knees feel weak and
she leans against a wooden shelf. "I will take this one," she says
timidly.

"Twelve-hundred rupees for Kali."

She knows the price must be too high. But can you barter for
a god? She simply opens her small purse and hands over the bills
without protest. The clerk wraps Kali and Caroline takes her and
steps onto the busy street.

Outside, Krishna flags down a motorized rickshaw and negoti-
ates the price. When the deal is done, he turns to Caroline. "He will
take us there."

She settles into the narrow space beside him. The driver
swerves down a narrow alley and out of the village then along a

new stretch of paved road that follows the river. Water is scarce and the land cracked and parched under the sun's infernal gaze. The broad river bed where torrents once flowed holds a narrow trickle of water. Washerwomen clean garments and spread them out along the sandy riverbed to dry.

"I don't think I came this far," Caroline says.

"Have you heard of the wish-fulfilling tree? Many people come to see it." He points up a hillside above the river bank.

Caroline turns her attention from the women scrubbing textiles at the river back to him. "What's that?"

"A saint who lived here many years ago gave discourses there. Sometimes he let people wish for the fruit they wanted and then it would appear in the branches of the tree. Some wanted cherries; others asked for oranges or mangos. The same tree bore all of these different fruits."

"Hum," Caroline says. "I don't know what I would have wished for. It seems that I've wished for so much, but never for the right things." She exhales a puff of exasperation and her eyes follow the bank up the hillside. "Do you believe in miracles?"

The rickshaw taxi stops and Krishna points down an alleyway. He indicates a sign, Prashanthi Hotel, with a red arrow pointing down the street. "It must be this one. Does this area look familiar?"

"I believe so."

"We'll soon find out."

The landscape wears barren, rocky hills singed black from the heat; yellow, withered weeds adorn the edge of the road, and cracked reddish-brown earth rises in clouds of dust then falls to cloak houses, beasts and people alike. Forsaken land with little water to sustain it. If she could peer inside and photograph her emotional landscape, the picture would look like this. Arid, desolate, dry. But soon it will turn green. The rains come during the monsoon and this world changes entirely. She pulls her knees up and hugs them to her chest, like a sitting foetus staring out into a harsh world, protected in the back seat of the wavering, weaving rickshaw. Sometimes it is good to turn back inside and see the bareness and the muddle.

This morning in a rare moment of sleep, she dreamed of walking into her living room – a dingy basement filled with clutter, chairs turned over, papers and books strewn about, dirty walls and carpets. When she came back later, light streamed in; the walls were white. A bouquet of roses sat in a crystal vase on the central table and the chairs were aligned as if waiting for an orchestra to come to play a concerto in perfect harmony. A woman stood at her side beaming. Was she the one who cleaned it up? "But I liked it the way it was," Caroline protested and then awoke.

A breeze stirs and exposes the underside of the leaves. She sighs. I felt comfortable with the mess, she thinks. It's hard to change, even if the new place promises to be better. Dark clouds gather on the horizon and the wind picks up. The washerwomen stop and point into the sky and seem to waver and wonder about what to do. When the first fat drops of water fall, they scurry around jerking up the neatly laid out clothes, placing them in baskets on their heads.

"It's raining," Caroline says with excitement.

"But it's not monsoon season!" Krishna says bewildered.

More drops fall. "Please stop. Please let me out." As a child, she played in the warm summer rains with delight, dancing and laughing and swaying under the generous silver streams. How long ago...how she has longed to grow. She steps into the rain as it descends in garlands, pearling down into the ground, dancing on her skin. A crowd of children erupt into laughter and run joyously under the downpour holding out round metal pots to capture it. Caroline holds out her hands, opens her palms to the sky, raises her face to the clouds and opens the vessel of her heart. Water cascades through her hair and drenches her skin as she whirls and laughs with the children to welcome the gentle rain.

Gratitude Page

Riviera Stories took shape over a year as I wrote a new story each month and shared it with friends. Thank you to those friends who contributed valuable feedback and for your kindness and support as this book took shape. Thanks also to Wanda Huntley who proofread the final version of this book. I love the Riviera and the significant role it played in my life. To the *Côte d'Azur*, the sea, and the beautiful people who lived and visited there, thank you for the inspiration and creative energy. I would also like to express gratitude to you, the readers, who like me, love to travel and explore the world, both inner and outer, through books.

Garden of Bliss
Cultivating the Inner Landscape for Self-Discovery
Debra Moffitt

"Like *Eat, Pray, Love* without the whine!"
—Janna McMahan, bestselling author of *Anonymity* and
The Ocean Inside

Garden of Bliss begins on the French Riviera, where Debra Moffitt, despite her glamorous lifestyle, feels empty. Realizing that financial success doesn't equal happiness, she looks inside herself and decides to make some changes.

Join Moffitt on a transformative path, where she invites you to nurture this metaphorical secret garden in order to discover a blissful life. Journey to your secret garden of bliss, a protected place of spirit and imagination where you can connect with your emotions, trust your insights, and rediscover peace. If you choose to explore your garden of bliss, a world of adventure opens within this sacred inner place of wisdom.

"If you are feeling depleted and spent, Debra Moffitt gently guides you to your inner space to refresh and inspire a serene state of joy, awakening, and creativity. *Garden of Bliss* is a must-read in today's harried world."

—Mary Alice Monroe, *New York Times* bestselling author of *Beach House Memories*

Published by Llewellyn Worldwide.
978-0-7387-3382-1, 288 pp, $ 16.99

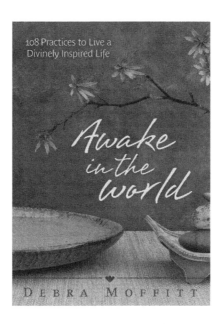

Awake in the World
108 Ways to Live a Divinely Inspired Life
Debra Moffitt

Everyone needs an anchor in this fast-paced and chaotic world. *Awake in the World* offers 108 simple ways to weave soul-nourishing peace and divinity into each day.

The engaging and practical guide was inspired by the author's own personal quest for spiritual enrichment. The practices she brought back from a journey around the world changed her life – and can transform yours. Drawn from an array of wisdom traditions, these 108 bite-sized exercises involving meditation, labyrinth walking, inspired lovemaking, mantras, and ritual – are quick and simple to do. By sharpening your spiritual awareness you'll learn to cultivate calm in a crisis, focus on what is truly important, and recognize the divine in everyday life. To support and encourage you on this exciting journey of self-discovery, the author shares her own personal, moving stories.

"Whatever your life situation and spiritual leanings, this book contains the most nutritious spiritual food from down through the centuries."—Sarah Susanka, bestselling author of *The Not So Big Life*

"Debra Moffitt brings the noble and universal yearnings of the human soul down to earth. This is ancient wisdom made accessible."—David Kundtz, bestselling author of *Quiet Mind*

Published by Llewellyn Worldwide.
978-0-7387-2722-6, 433 pp. 5x7 $16.95

Made in United States
Orlando, FL
07 March 2022

15524691R00115